I0737998

REVELATION

JOHN IRVIN

Other works by John Irvin:

<u>Longevity Series</u>
Revelation
Independence (Coming 2020)
<u>StarQuest Anthology:</u>
Forgetfulness
Epix
StarQuest (A Novel)
<u>Mermaid Seas (A Novelette Anthology):</u>
Discovery
Forecast
Salvation
<u>Shatters (A Short Story Serial):</u>
Collapse
Revolt
Anarchy
Spark
Conspiracy (Coming Soon)
<u>Kindle Romance Novellas</u>
Even When We're Ghosts
All The Reasons Why
As the Sun Will Rise
Can't Help Falling(Coming Soon)
<u>Children of Alia series</u>
The King
The Medallion (Coming Soon)
<u>Other Stories</u>
Doom Through The Rabbit Hole
Pochatok
Wolf's Rising
Blood of the Father

LONGEVITY REVELATION

JOHN IRVIN

IngramSpark

© Copyright 2019 John Irvin. All rights reserved.

No part of this book may be reproduced, stored in a retrieval system, or transmitted by any means without the written permission of the author.

Published by Ingram Spark

Printed in United States of America.

Cover Art by

Cherie Fox
www.cheriefox.com

To Debbie, you gave the spark that
became this world.

CONTENTS

1

When the cold jagged touch brushed his neck, Ihon Iraes woke with a start. His body remaining as still as a corpse, he allowed his eyelids to open just a crack. Breathing in the scents around him, he took in the information.

According to his nostrils, there were four men.

One held the knife to Ihon's throat, the other three were rummaging around his campsite.

He was alone, traveling home from political debates in Edinburgh over the Clans.

There wasn't much the thieves could take, except the bearskin blanket on top of him or the diminutive morsels in his saddle—well, okay, his horse was the most valuable thing he had with him, they could steal that.

Not my horse, his mind protested. Not Cassieus. That old war steed was akin to his best friend, having served him so many years all over the known world.

"I'm surprised this bloke hasn't awakened," the man with the knife called out to his companions, his voice was raspy.

Ihon remained still, his right hand inching over to the five-foot Scottish Claymore lying at his right side, opposite the thief. The tips of his fingers finally touched the cold steel and slipped around the blade.

There was no time to worry about finding the hilt.

Grabbing the two-edged metal, Ihon opened wide his eyes.

The man with the knife let out a gasp, startled by his victim's dark brown eyes glaring up at him. He was about to say something, yell to his friends, when his face turned to the sword now swinging down at him.

The blade hacked into the thief's left shoulder, sending him sprawling on the ground next to Ihon.

Thrusting himself up onto his feet, Ihon yanked his Claymore back, before bringing it down again, this time ending the man's life by severing his neck from the back.

The head plopped onto the ground, blood spurted from the open esophagus while the body crumpled forward as if bowing to some deity.

"Caynan?" One of the other men jumped, gaping at the sight.

"I do believe Caynan has met his Maker by now," Ihon muttered, standing up to his full six feet. Brushing the wave of nausea that threatened to send him hurling, he brandished his sword.

"You a Crusader?" One of the other two muggers questioned. He was thick-set man with a long raven braid dangling from his neck. He studied Ihon with the scrutiny of a seasoned fighter.

Ihon glared back, his thick eyebrows lowering in a scowl—he knew this past war with the Muslim kingdoms had left distaste in the mouth of most, so he was ready for an onslaught of verbal abuse.

"What's it to you?" He retorted, sniffing the air.

His nose had always had a knack for sensing certain bodily scents.

Glancing toward the second thief, he bared his teeth and watched the man squirm.

The stench of warm urine met Ihon's nostrils.

"I fought in the war myself," the first man replied. "The Second Crusade was a bitter defeat to Christendom."

"Some would say that," Ihon muttered, returning his gaze to the speaker. "Others might say, we gained an advantage, a foothold in the Holy Land. After four hundred years of slaughter by those black hearts, I would think that a victory."

The first man shrugged, standing to his feet, he tossed the pack he'd been exploring to the ground next to Ihon's horse.

The battle steed blew his nose. Taking a step forward, Cassieus gave a bit of a whinny to his master.

"You're horse seems to want to join the fight, Sir Knight," First man remarked. He glanced toward the midnight-coloured stallion, a bit nervous.

"Maybe," Ihon let the smile tease his mouth. "Then again, sometimes he just enjoys watching a good skirmish."

"Can we get on with this now?" The second man, an obvious stain the size of a hand marking the crotch of his trousers, shuffled a few steps to his right.

"What's the matter, Ferrick," the First man glanced at his partner. "You afraid to end up like Caynan? Our friend was stupid. Never put a knife to the throat of a Crusader. Isn't that right, Sir Knight?"

"Tis true," Ihon bared his teeth. "And before I send you and your friend to join Caynan in meeting our Blessed Redeemer, what are your names? I am Sir Ihon Iraes, son of Sir Justin Iraes."

"You have spirit, Sir Ihon," the First man chuckled. "I am Thomas Brent, son of Sir Walter Brent. This is my cowardly partner in crime, Ferrick Gant, his father is of no importance."

"Good to know," Ihon side-stepped, twirling the blade of his Scottish claymore outward. His left hand held back the untied girth of his kilt, keeping it from falling around his legs.

The tension mounted, sending each man's pulse into overdrive.

Ferrick let loose a war cry — sounding more like a shrieking hag than a knight charging into battle.

The blade of the attacker batted the air, just inches from Ihon's left arm.

Spinning on his heels, Ihon brought his own sword up to meet the biting metal. He grinned like a savage, making sure to meet the frightened thief's gaze. His nostrils flaring, he could smell the terror now oozing through Ferrick's pores.

At that moment, Thomas decided to jump in. His weapon was a black-bladed dirk, the length of an average man's forearm. With a quick dash, he plunged the exaggerated dagger forward and up, hoping the pointed end would meet the flesh between Ihon's third and fourth ribs.

Spinning like lightning, the veteran Crusader swung his Claymore in an arc. He aimed for Thomas's stab.

The razor edge of his sword sliced a gash across Ferrick's chest before it bit into Thomas's left bicep.

A groan escaped Thomas's mouth while Ferrick cried.

Sniveling, the weaker dropped to his knees and threw his own weapon away.

The tool landed with a clang against a stone in the dirt.

Thomas, however, growled and maintained his balance. He clenched his teeth and glared at his opponent. Blood squirting from his wound, he dropped his eyes to where he'd shoved his dirk.

Ihon raised an eyebrow as he too turned his gaze to the smaller weapon.

The blade managed to cut an inch through the leather vest he was wearing, barely biting the flesh underneath.

Thomas grinned as he started to push his fists against the elongated dagger.

Ihon grimaced. But he turned sideways again and swatted his foe's head with his left hand.

The impact knocked Thomas off of his feet and he tripped. Landing with a thud on the ground, he rolled over onto his back, jumping back to his feet. Gripping his left arm with his right hand, he searched the area.

He'd dropped his dirk and couldn't see it in the flickering glow of the dying campfire.

"Excellent work, I must say," Ihon pursed his lips. He could feel the flesh in his side closing up already — something he'd noticed during the war on many occasions, always thinking it odd.

Thomas finally caught sight of his weapon and dove forward.

Ihon jumped in its direction as well but he didn't reach it in time.

With a laugh, Thomas staggered to his feet, brandishing the blade again. It was then that he realised, he was standing only three steps away from his still-blubbering partner's sword. One quick hop and he was able to reach down and pick it up. Waving both weapons in front of him, he chuckled.

"You may be good, Crusader, but now I have twice as many blades as you."

"And I have God Almighty," Ihon responded, arching an eyebrow while angling his head. "Tell me, how do you deal with the Sword of Vengeance?"

Thomas raised both eyebrows, hesitating.

It was in that fraction of a second, when the thief's guard was down, his blades lowering just an inch, that his defenses were opened.

Ihon charged, his frame looking more like blur.

When the blade entered his heart, Thomas didn't realise it. But when the Claymore protruded out through his back, it dawned on him, he would see eternity in a matter of seconds.

A gasp jumped from his lips.

Eyes glazing over, Thomas faced the victor. He wanted to say something, but couldn't think of anything when the cold climbed up his arms and legs. He felt dizzy.

Ihon watched, his face grim. He'd been reluctant to throw that last move.

Thomas stumbled, his mouth gaped open, face turning ashen.

As the body collapsed sideways, Ihon pulled his blade out, wincing at the sound the tearing flesh made. Pausing for a moment, he glanced up at the starry sky. Then, he turned to focus on Ferrick.

The man was now on all fours, eyes widened in horror at the spectacle before him, mouth hanging open.

"Go home," Ihon growled. His stomach felt as if it were rolling over and twisting itself up in knots with his intestines. "Go home and don't ever thieve again."

"As you command, good Knight," Ferrick muttered, snot dangling from his nose, spit dribbling down his chin as he spoke. "I won't ever steal again, I promise. On my own life, good Knight, I swear. Thank you for your mercy."

"Go!" Ihon roared, his left hand waving the bleating creature away. Certain he was about to upchuck at the man's cowardice, he shut his eyes and gritted his teeth until the sound of the former thief's feet finally dissipated into the night.

Cassieus whinnied, he'd been quiet the entire time. Walking forward, his shod feet clapping against the dirt, he shook his large head.

Ihon opened his eyes, reaching up to pat the horse's forehead. He then ran his fingers through the flowing mane.

"Yes, my friend," he breathed. "It's over."

The steed nodded in affirmation. He gave a loud snort before nuzzling the tired knight's shoulder.

"I'm exhausted, Cassieus," Ihon chuckled as he leaned his cheek against the warm horse cheek. "But with all this adrenaline in my veins, thanks to those fools, I couldn't grab another wink if it were the Last Day. Might as well pack up and head out."

Cassieus neighed.

"You like that idea, old friend?" Ihon grinned, pulling back to look the stallion in the eye. "It does mean we'll be home sooner. By the blood, that means I'll see my lovely Joanna. Oh what a blessed day this will be!"

With that thought sending a thrill like an electric charge through his entire nervous system, Ihon poked around his campsite. Throwing everything together and shoving it into his saddle bags, he saddled his battle steed and started off.

A streak of red could be seen on the horizon by the time the travelers began their day's trip northward across the midland hills of the Dark Island.

"Ah, Scotland," Ihon closed his eyes and breathed deeply. "How I love your bonnie heather-filled air."

Cassieus trotted a little quicker, seeming to agree with his rider's statement.

The highlands were a legendary sight. The ancients told stories of its dark and mysterious regions. Some folks claimed it was nothing but a treacherous realm holding death or a dismal existence for anyone stupid enough to live among the lochs and mountains.

But others relished the magical lustiness of Scotland's northern lands.

Ihon was one of those adoring fools.

Steps sending echoes out across an open valley below them, Cassieus ascended the rocky path carved into the side of a mountain.

Peasants traveling from the outer clans to a nearby village had cut the road centuries ago. It wasn't as dangerous as it used to be, though time and wind had worn it down in some places.

The knight clenched his teeth when his eyes dropped to his right and saw the dive of the cliff just a couple feet away.

Cassieus shivered, snorting.

Ihon laughed, "Nervous, old boy? Or was that a laugh."

The war horse kept plodding forward.

Though it seemed to take forever, the travelers reached the highest point of the narrow road before the sun managed to climb to the peak of its own ascent in the sky.

A smile broke across Ihon's face as he took in the ravishing sight that stretched out for miles before him.

On the horizon, the gleaming edge of the sea to the west could be glimpsed. Northward was an army of monstrous, yet beautiful, mountains jutting across the stretch of land. But between them and the travelers was a valley.

The valley wrapped around the feet of the mountains for the length of near five miles toward the east. At its center was a crescent hill. To the west was a lake reaching half a mile until it disappeared behind another mountain.

Set just beyond the crescent hill was a group of man-made structures.

At this distance, Ihon could just barely make out the difference between his house and barn. But he knew it was them.

"We'll be there by the time my sweet Joanna has supper ready, Cassieus," Ihon wanted to jump off his saddle and fly into the sky in order to make it home sooner. He kicked his heels into the horse's sides and clucked his tongue.

2

Even as Cassieus climbed the crescent hill standing between him and everything making his home, Ihon could smell that scent that always impelled his heart into a skipping rhythm.

The smell reminded him of a dash of honey with rose petals. No perfumes produced this, it was natural. It was her scent.

Joanna Iraes, his wife, formerly a Wallace from the nearby clan, had held him in matrimonial bliss for twenty-five years.

"Can't believe a month has passed since I've held her in my arms," Ihon spoke to his horse. "I feel as if it's been an eternity. How in the worlds did I ever survive being away from her for years during the Second Crusade?"

The horse snorted, acting bored of his master's ramble. He trotted a bit until reaching the top of the hill. Pausing, the aged battle stallion took in the sights.

Ihon knew his grin probably looked so boyish, but he didn't care. His eyes ran from the stone house, across the fenced barnyard, and to the wooden barn, when he let his smile widen even more.

The barn door opened, sounds of chickens cackling springing from inside.

Ihon caught his breath as he watched her step forth—she reminded him of a goddess stepping out onto the back of a cloud in an old Greek play he'd seen while in Edinburgh for the past month.

Draped in a dark blue, cloth-stitched dress, Joanna carried a basket of eggs against her waist. She plodded through the mud along the wooden fence of the yard in the direction of the two-story house.

Ihon realised he was still holding his breath. Taking in a deep gasp, he kicked his mount again.

Cassieus barely needed prodding. Charging forward, he tore down the hill.

Joanna froze mid-step before turning to peer in their direction. A grin cut across her face as she set the basket of eggs on the top of the closest fence post. She brushed her dark golden brown hair out of her face and started forward.

Ihon reigned in his over-eager steed before there was a chance of splattering his wife with mud. A laugh sprung from his lips while he leaped the rest of the way.

She jumped up into his arms, wrapping her own arms around his neck.

Lifting her up, till her feet dangled in the air, Ihon spun around, twirling her.

She squealed and clung tighter. Then, when he stopped spinning, she planted her mouth on his lips. Eyes slamming shut, she breathed in his musk while plunging her tongue under his.

Ihon smiled as he returned the kiss. He felt a smoldering heat begin burning his chest, sending tingling electricity down his arms and sizzling in his fingertips. Rolling his tongue around hers, he growled.

Pulling out, Joanna raised her eyebrows and looked at him.

"Missed me that much, you beastly knight?" She purred. Her right hand moved up his neck, entangling her fingers in his shoulder-length dark brown hair. She pecked his lips, loving the tickle his thick beard gave her chin.

"Aye, bonnie wife," he winked. "I've been starving something awful for your touch."

"Well," Joanna cradled his head in her arms, kissing both cheeks before continuing. "Put up old Cassieus in the barn, wash yourself, and I'll have supper ready for you to quench your hunger."

"But it is you I hunger for more, my love," Ihon moaned. He stared into her russet brown eyes, wishing he could dive into their depths and live there forever.

"Aye, ye will have me," she breathed on his nose. Her lips brushed the top of his beard before gliding over his lips again. "After ye've eaten, you need strength for what I've planned for tonight."

That last sentence empowered the heat.

Ihon couldn't help but growl a second time. He dropped her on her feet and made a mad dash the few feet back to his waiting horse.

Joanna laughed loudly. She shook her head, hands on her hips, while she watched her husband lead the old mount into the barn. Then, with a sigh, she picked up the basket of eggs and headed inside the house.

Meanwhile, Ihon unbuckled the stirrups and hoisted the saddle off of his horse's back. Tossing it onto a post, he turned back to Cassieus and gave the stallion a quick brush.

His stomach growled.

Cassieus snorted, glancing sideways at his master.

Ihon was certain he saw a teasing stare in the gaze. He grinned and shrugged. Motioning to the wooden trough that held some hay, he remarked.

"If you were married, you'd understand." He hurried over to the wall and lifted a pitch fork off its mantel. In a matter of minutes, he had a good load of fresh hay waiting for the war horse's dinner.

"There ya go, ole boy," Ihon patted Cassieus's neck as he tossed the pitch fork against the back wall. "Eat up. You have a good night as well. As for me, I'm going to have some home-made supper. If that wife of mine knows me, she'll have a good pot of lamb stew waiting for me."

With that he gave one last pat before stepping outside and shutting the barn door behind him.

The glow of candlelight from inside flickered through an open window of the stone house.

The structure was not average in the Highlands. Most visitors—rare they be—often commented on how much like a small castle it appeared. With two stories and a small tower, Ihon and Joanna agreed.

Ihon had built it shortly before leaving for the Second Crusade.

Nearly skipping the rest of the way to the front door, Ihon knocked on the old oak.

The door swung open and Joanna stood their in a newly-made green gown.

"You crazy old fool," she grinned while shaking her head at him. Grabbing his arm, she ushered him in. "You don't need to knock."

"Old fool?" Ihon paused just inside as she shut the door behind him. "I'm not old, my love."

"You are nearing fifty years, dear husband," the brunette set her hands on her hips and straightened to her full five feet and seven inches.

"Aye," Ihon let out a heavy sign. "Tis true. Not much time left, do I?"

Joanna's face darkened but just for a brief moment. She shook her head and grinned again, but there were obvious lines of sadness under her eyes on her high cheekbones.

Ihon quickly grabbed her waist and pulled her to him. Bending his head down, he pressed his lips to hers and ground down—not painful, just passionate.

She met his zeal with the fiery blaze that can only be found in the heart of a Scottish woman. This came from blood lines dating back to the Celts and the Picts, along with the true Scots that first settled ancient Caledonia.

The kiss seemed to last for quite an hour before the couple pulled away and turned to the supper table.

Ihon's mouth watered and his stomach growled again at the sight and smell of the delicious roasted lamb chops stuffed into the dark stew pot.

"You know me so well," he smiled, sitting down at the head of the table.

Joanna picked up his wooden bowl and dumped three loads of the stew into it with her ladle. She then seated herself and gave herself two scoops.

Ihon devoured the bowl's contents in minutes. He took a second helping of his own accord and was halfway finished with that when Joanna spoke up.

"Do you mind not wearing that sword at the supper table, Ihon?"

Ihon paused. He glanced at her then over his shoulder at the hilt of his claymore sticking up behind his back. He chuckled.

"I totally forgot I was wearing it."

Standing to his feet, he unbuckled the strap of the sheath and lifted it off his back. Walking over to the wall next to the front door, he laid the weapon across two sets of deer antlers nailed in between the stones.

"She's a glorious work, don't ya believe, my love?" He grinned.

"Aye," Joanna nodded. "Now come back and finish your supper."

"As you wish," he returned. Sitting down, he continued to hold the sword in his gaze for a moment. Eyes dreamy, he gave a contented sigh.

"Father knew what he was doing when he crafted it. Mother told me, when she gave it to me, he'd built it out of the strongest metals from Rome."

Joanna nodded, obviously deep in thought now.

"It would be amazing if my parents could have become friends with yours. They would have hit it off so well, I do believe."

"I do too, dear," Joanna smiled, reaching over to clasp his hand with hers. "I was wondering though, what war did your father fight in? Was it the first Crusade? I barely remember much of that war."

"Nay," Ihon shook his head. "Mother says it was a great war but came well before the first Crusade. She never mentioned much about it. I do know it was in that war that Father passed away."

Both of them gazed at the sword again. They studied the etchings on the hilt that made up the Iraes family crest.

It was a full moon with a wolf's head cut into its center. Wrapped around the circle was a vine-like branch with a strange flower. Then carved into the base of the crest was the Roman number MDCCXVII.

"Have you ever figured out what those numbers signify?" Joanna questioned.

"No," Ihon turned back to his bowl of stew and shook his head. "I don't think I'm even close. Mother never told me—she was always mysterious about the crest and our Roman origins."

A moment passed before he continued a thought out loud.

"My father was able to pass that sword down to me," he paused, mind searching for the right words. "I long to pass it down to my son."

Joanna pushed back in her chair. Standing up, she grabbed her bowl and his and tossed them into the barrel where dirty dishes went. In the morning, she'd take the barrel on her morning errand to the lake down on the other end of the valley.

"Calab isn't with us anymore," she muttered, bitterness dripping from her lips.

Ihon grimaced. Apparently, he'd said the wrong words.

3

All the worlds in all the galaxies cannot substitute for the loss of a loved one. If anyone knew loss, the Iraes family had its share.

"My dear sweet Love," Ihon stood to his feet and slid around the table. He reached for his wife. "Forgive me, I did not wish to bring up that cursed memory."

Joanna stood hovering over the dirty dishes barrel. Her back to him, she crossed her arms over her chest.

Ihon stepped up behind her and encircled her with his arms just under hers. He pulled her to him and leaned his face into her hair. Breathing her scent in deeply, he closed his eyes for a moment. With a smack of his lips, he kissed the back of her head before letting out a sigh.

She rested her head against his shoulder, closing her eyes.

His gaze fell to the creamy skin of her neck. Roving down to her collar bone, which the green hand-sewn dress revealed—in fact, its neckline started at her left shoulder and swooped down in front dipping under her right arm.

The flickering candles and the fire in the hearth just inside the connected den, sent a shadow in that space above her collar bone.

Ihon smiled and lowered his head. Resting his lips in that shadowy patch of skin, he breathed on her.

Joanna's eyes fluttered as a heat rushed up her neck. She felt the fire burning in her cheeks. But the pain in her gut was still heavy.

"We should never have taken Calab and Susan to Rome," she winced, it hurt to say those two names.

Ihon gritted his teeth, pulling his mouth away from her shoulder. He let go of her waist and shifted on his heels. Shaking his head, he couldn't find an answer, at least one that was worthy.

"If we hadn't taken them when you went to try to find your father's relatives, they wouldn't be dea—they wouldn't be gone."

"Joanna," Ihon's voice was husky. He waited till she pivoted her body around to face him. "There is nothing we can change about the past. When those assassins murdered our beautiful children that night, I lost a part of me just as I know you did too. But they are in the arms of our Lord and Saviour—there is no safer place to be."

"But they could have grown up and had families of their own."

"Yes," Ihon grimaced, turning away from his wife. "They could have. But they didn't. We need to move on."

"I will never move on," Joanna stated this with such a fury, her tone almost cut into a scream.

Ihon studied her, he wished he could take her pain away. But how could he do that when the same pain was cutting his own heart? Yes, he would never let go of his children's memories, but he also decided a long time ago he wouldn't let that stop him from dreaming of more children and raising them up to adulthood to take on this sick, dark world.

"I just can't think about having anymore right now," Joanna took a step toward him. She knew he was hurting too. Keeping her eyes focused on the collar of his tunic under his kilt, she reached out and rested her right hand on his chest. She could just barely make out the beat of his heart beneath her touch.

"Let's move into the den, my Love," he took her hand and led her into the next room. They stopped near the stone fireplace and studied the lapping flames.

Stretched out in the middle of the floor was a large bear-skin rug, complete with the animal's snarling head. Its chestnut brown fur had blanketed the oaken floor ever since Ihon slew the creature near ten years ago, not many years after he'd built the house.

They cuddled on the couch they built together out of an old pine nearly three years prior.

Joanna closed her eyes, leaning her head against his shoulder.

Ihon smiled and rested his cheek against the top of her head. He pulled her shoulders closer into his embrace while he watched the fire dance on the hearth.

"So, you have yet to tell me how the meetings in Edinburgh went," Joanna spoke up, breaking the silence.

Ihon let out a heavy sigh, he did not want to speak of the events of the past month.

"That exciting, huh?" His wife chuckled, pulling away far enough to take in his face.

"Well," he pursed his lips. Reaching up with his free hand, he scratched the beard on his jaw. "Just the regular, politics, clan feuds, possible future heirs to the Throne of Scotland. Boring, boring, boring."

Joanna giggled and patted her husband on the top of his head.

"There, there, my darling, it's all over."

Ihon grinned and honed his gaze in on her lips. He did not want to think of world events. He wanted to taste those lips again, to taste her tongue. He'd gone a month without the heat of his wife's body entangled around his.

"Why do the clans have to feud so much? We are supposed to be a nation. We have a king, how come Malcolm the Fourth can't straighten them out?"

Ihon let a growl escape his lips. He rolled his eyes and grabbed his wife by her shoulders.

"Whatever is the matter, dear?" Joanna raised both her eyebrows, but there was a teasing twinkle in her russet eyes. Something twitched at the corner of her lips.

Shaking his head, Ihon yanked her to him and enveloped her lips with his mouth.

A giggle jumped from her mouth into his.

She then closed her eyes with a tiny moan.

The electricity sizzled up Ihon's arms and he was sure his heart was suddenly lit on fire. Feeling the heat flush his cheeks, he plunged his tongue under hers.

Joanna smiled against his lips, her hands gliding up his arms to cup his cheeks. She twisted her tongue around his in a wet dance. Judging from the heat in her face, she knew she probably looked as red as a tomato.

Ihon's hands moved from her shoulders down to her sides. He shifted his wait until he was sprawled out almost on top of her.

She invited this move, moving her body under him, loving the security this brought to her being. How she had missed this warm safety now enveloping her. Too many nights she worried he might never return, leaving her alone in the dark highlands.

But together they could weather any storm, fight away any shadow.

At least, that's what the two of them believed, their bodies beginning to writhe in passion while their tongues danced with each other.

4

Racing pulses, hearts beating in perfect rhythm, the two married lovers clung to each other.

With a gasp, Ihon pulled away, catching himself before he fell off the pinewood couch. He chuckled as he stared down into her eyes, his own gaze smoldering. Every nerve in his body felt like it was being consumed by the raging heat of his passion for her.

His right hand reached up and caressed the skin of her bared shoulder, pulling the top of the gown down just a few inches at first.

He studied the necklace that draped her neck. A smile spread his lips apart when he recalled the day he'd found that silver chain in a market and bought it for her.

Hanging from the silver chain was a round silver pendant holding a blue sapphire with green specks filling its depths.

His nostrils flared, taking in her scent.

Something ice cold caught in the back of his neck sending a sliver of goose bumps down his spine.

He'd smelled something else.

Something dark — make that malevolent.

Noticing the sudden catch of his eyebrows, the quick tightening of his lips, Joanna cocked her head. Peering up at him, she lifted her right eyebrow. Before she could ask what was wrong, she felt his hand draped across her mouth.

He then raised his index finger to his lips. Turning his head just slightly, he edged himself up in order to look over the top of the couch.

The large casement window beyond the den opened a view of the crescent hill outside in the night.

But the glow from the hearth's fire did not allow much visibility.

Sniffing the air, Ihon rolled one leg off the couch, his bare foot touching the wooden floor.

Someone was in the house — or some thing, he couldn't figure it out. He'd never smelled this odour before. For some reason, the only word that kept coming to mind with the scent was: cursed.

But what was cursed? He clenched his jaws. He hated that his sword was on the other side of the doorway.

"What is it?" Joanna sat up.

Ihon waved his left hand at her, motioning for silence again. Taking a step forward, he moved to the doorway leading into the foyer. If he could make it to his sword, he could ward away whatever it was that was hiding in the shadows nearby.

Joanna watched, eyebrows drawn in concern. Reaching up, she pulled the neckline of her gown back up to her shoulder.

Inching into the other room, Ihon's eyes searched the darker interior. His hand moved up the wall until it clasped the waiting weapon lying across the antlers. With a quick twist of his wrist, the blade was dangling in his hand. He clutched the leather-bound handle and pivoted on his heels.

Just a few feet to his right was the staircase leading up to the second floor which held the master bedroom and the viewing tower.

But before he could even think of approaching the first step, the lights exploded in his head. He grunted while the room spun like lightning around him. Toppling to the floor, he heard a blood-curdling scream echo in the distance just before everything went black.

~

The cold oak pressed against his cheek as Ihon blinked his eyes open. His head ached with the worst headache he'd ever had. Reaching up with a grunt, he grazed his fingers against the back of his head.

The hair was wet with something warm.

Lifting his head as he brought his hand in front of his face, he gaped through blurry eyes.

His fingers were covered in dark blood—it could be black, he'd seen it before. Though he'd thought it strange the first few times he'd seen it during the Second Crusade's many battles, he'd grown accustomed to its darkness.

Something warped the skin just below his bottom right rib.

Reaching down, he ran his finger along a wound — well, it used to be a wound. Apparently, after knocking him out, someone had stabbed him. But the wound was nearly healed already.

Sitting up with a start, he gasped, the memories surged back. He'd been hit in the head form behind. How long he was out, he couldn't tell.

It was still night so probably not too long.

Then, the echo of a scream bounced inside his head.

"Joanna," he growled, jumping to his feet. Spinning around, he charged into the den, sword twirling in his hands. He would kill if anyone hurt her.

What awaited him in the next room sent his world spiraling into chaos.

Ihon's feet froze under him, the momentum from his rush sending him to his knees.

There she lay, stretched out in the middle of the room across the bear rug. On her back, her head lolled over, she stared at the wall a few yards away, unmoving.

"No," Ihon could barely breathe. He reached for her, fingers hesitating an inch above her head. Feeling like someone had driven a pronged spear into his gut and twisted, he ran his fingers down her cheek.

The blood on her chest was only partially dried, it inched down to the floor beneath her neck from the jagged gash that ran in a crescent shape below her throat. The silver necklace was blotched with crimson stains.

"No," was the only word able to drop from his mouth while his fingers ran through her hair.

If the walls collapsed in a heap of rubble around him, it would still not match the shattering world inside his soul. His mind was caving while his heart crumbled into shards.

Who did this? What kind of monster would murder such an innocent, beautiful creature?

The broken pieces of his heart lit into fire, grief twisting into rage.

Jumping to his feet, Ihon let a deep growl rise in his throat, he jumped over the couch, sword bared along with his teeth. He dashed through the casement window, barely noticing when the glass shattered around him.

"Where are you?" He roared, heaving. Eyes searching his surroundings, he sniffed the air.

There was no trace of the assassin.

Ihon's face was twitching like mad now. He gritted his teeth.

What is going on? His mind screamed.

He gasped for air, it was like something inside was wanting out. Holding it in was starting to get painful.

Panting for air, Ihon cringed when a wave of tingling swept from the tips of his fingers up his arms.

Same thing happened to his toes, straight up his legs.

It felt good.

He did not want to feel good right now. The aching in his chest was more than he could bear. He wanted to find the murderer and rip him — or her — to shreds.

Joanna.

With a heartbroken growl, Ihon rushed back inside and jumped over the couch, nearly knocking it over with his feet. Plunging to the floor next to her body, Ihon reached up with both hands and cupped her face between them. Body racked with sobs, he bent over and kissed her lips.

They were already cold.

"My love," he groaned, another wave sent an icy chill over his entire body. "Come back to me."

Joanna's eyes were empty.

Shutting his own eyes, Ihon covered hers with his left hand. With his right hand, he lifted her chin. He brushed his nose against hers.

The tears poured from his eyes down her face.

"My love," he breathed her endearment through the weeping. His hand dropped to her chest, fingers tracing the silver chain of the necklace.

A bolt of sizzling energy arched his spine.

He cried out, clutching the chain. Pulling it off her neck, he gripped it as if his life depended on it.

Bones realigned, muscles contorted beneath his skin. His body shivered, feeling like the very pores were multiplying and growing.

Ihon blanched, his eyes dropping to his hands.

The fingers and thumbs spread out at unnatural angles before realigning into larger digits. The skin started to darken. It took a moment, but in a matter of seconds, it dawned on him, they weren't darkening but instead were growing an otherworldly amount of hair.

The hair growth rippled up over his arms and covered his entire body like waves of darkness. Next a thick pelt of black fur sprung over his shoulders and chest, reaching down over his abdomen and crotch.

While all this was happening, to top it all off, his body grew in size.

The shirt beneath his kilt shredded into pieces of fabric. The kilt, no longer able to retain his frame, peeled off like an onion.

"What in the worlds is happening to me?" Ihon scared himself by the snarl he now spoke with. He stood to his feet.

The waves were gone, larger bones finishing up their changing.

His head felt heavier.

Reaching up, Ihon felt his face. He could see his nose, it was black and elongated. Grabbing his face, he scurried over to a mirror hanging on the wall in the corner to the fireplace's left. Nearly tripping over his enlarged feet, he froze when he came into view in the reflection.

"By the gods of the ancient," he muttered, catching himself halfway through when his voice came out deeper than he'd ever heard it.

The reflection gawked back at him. With the head of a wolf, larger than life, its dark eyes were human, staring back at him.

"Lord God, what am I?" He growled. Ever so slowly, he pulled himself away from the mirror. His world was spinning so fast he was certain he'd pass out in a second. When his eyes fell on Joanna's corpse, he groaned.

It came out as howl, rising from deep in his burning chest, climbing up his throat and freeing itself from his opened muzzle.

That has to be the strangest thing I've ever done, he thought to himself. What am I? Some kind of man wolf creature?

His tongue ran along his teeth.

"Ow!" He blurted out, tasting blood.

His teeth weren't your normal human dentures anymore. They were large and razor-sharp fangs.

Collapsing to his knees again at his wife's side, his head swayed. This was all too much for him. The loss of the love of his life and his changing into some kind of monster sent him sprawled out on the floor. He swung his arm over her stomach before the blackness took him again.

~

When his eyes cracked open, the sun was peaking in through the windows, filling the rooms with its radiant light. It was as if Sol had come to see what was wrong with the Iraes household.

Ihon reached up and rubbed his eyes. He kept them closed though, because he knew Joanna's dead body was still lying next to him, cold and stiff now. Sitting up, he realised he was still clutching the necklace in his hand.

Sometime during the night, he'd changed back into his human form.

Feeling bare and vulnerable, he sat there holding his gaze on the now dead coals in the fireplace at his feet.

"I swear, Joanna," he gritted his teeth. "I will find him, I will kill him. You will be avenged, my love." Finally gaining the courage, he turned to her figure and reached for her face. Brushing a strand of her hair out of her closed eyes, he swallowed the sobs threatening to take over again.

It was time to put her to rest outside next to those two headstones where they'd laid their two children together so many years ago.

"At least you're with them now," he smiled, almost choking.

A tear plunged over his eyelid down his cheek, followed by another then a third. In a minute, he let them flow, shoulders shaking as he moved her head into his lap and cradled her.

"Just a few more minutes, my love," he moaned. "Then I'll let you go to them."

Sol had climbed to the peak of his ascent in the sky outside by the time Ihon managed to finally dress his wife for burial. Putting her in her favourite dress, he then cleaned the dried blood off before lifting her in his arms and carrying her out the front door. Rounding the house, he forced one step after the other until he came to the small mound set next to a grove of pine trees.

Waiting there were two gray stones, hand-carved and etched with two names along with dates.

"Calab, Susan," Ihon paused at the foot of the graves, clinging to the stiff body in his arms. "You're mother has come home to you." He choked on a sob. "I can just see the three of you. Wish I was with you now."

The next hour was spent digging the new grave and laying her to rest. Finding a large stone in perfect shape nearby, he set it at the head. Carving her name and dates into the smooth face took up the rest of the afternoon.

When the sun dipped beneath the mountains and finally allowed dusk to begin its embrace of the sky, Ihon finished and headed back inside the empty house. A dark determination gripped his soul while he grabbed a couple packs and started filling them with an assortment of necessities.

Once finished, he then sheathed his sword, strapped the sheath to his back, and slung the pack over his left shoulder, hurrying through the front door. Making sure the old oak shut, he then turned and surveyed the crescent hill. Taking a whiff, he closed his eyes.

It was then when his nostrils caught the gagging odour.

5

Even Cassieus was perturbed at the smell.

Ihon scowled. He could feel his teeth itching to grow into those fangs he'd discovered the night before. Studying the trunk of the tree from atop his saddled mount, the kilted veteran allowed his mind to dream up hideous aspirations.

You murder my wife, his brain growled. And thinking you murdered me, you decide to take a piss on my land?

Cassieus shook his head and snorted several times — apparently as frustrated as his master.

After smelling the odour, Ihon had saddled the old war horse in a flash, riding him over the hill in its direction.

It was rank but no more than a day's old.

The assassin hadn't waited around for long — whether he'd seen the transformation of the human into a monster, Ihon wasn't sure.

"I will find you," Ihon called out into the last bit of dim light from dusk. "And you will wish you never heard my name."

Cassieus nodded and gave a clipped neigh while tapping the grassy dirt with his right front hoof.

"Are you ready, my friend?" Ihon couldn't help but smile through the tears still stinging his eyes. He then clucked his tongue and the two set out on their path of vengeance.

They did not rest. Only stopping to take a drink at a river, they pushed forward. When morning came along, they'd already passed the Loch Ness and would reach Edinburgh by the end of the day.

Along the way, Ihon caught sight of a spec of torn cloth. He could smell the murderer's strange scent all over it. A triumphant grin tickled the corners of his mouth as he led his horse southward.

"I do believe he's trying to find haven in a Lowland city," he mused, listening to a seagull crying overhead, giving her welcome to the morning sun. "That or he's making a break for the border. Perhaps he thinks that'll save him."

An ocean breeze wafted over the two hunters.

His own mane nearly matching that of his battle steed's, Ihon grinned—certain if anyone saw it, they'd think him mad, the way his teeth bared.

"No borders will keep me from having my vengeance."

Cassieus whinnied in affirmation.

They passed Edinburgh sometime during the night.

Only once for about half an hour did Cassieus need to stop and nap.

It dawned on Ihon he did not feel tired at all. Feeling like he could go on for days, he stared up at the moon hanging in the sky.

She stared down at him, the crescent of her shape was in its waxing phase.

Waking with a start, the horse spent a few minutes eating a small breakfast of heather and grass. He then took a swig of water from the water bag Ihon offered him.

Then they were off again.

"To the border, my friend," Ihon muttered, his mind was in deep tribulation. His eyes rose to the moon again, while he gripped the reins. Something inside him felt connected to that heavenly body.

The muscles in his arms and legs tensed for a brief second before relaxing again—he was certain they'd just grown in size and definition.

"What on earth," he breathed, raising one hand in front of his face and studied it like he'd never seen it before.

While he racked his mind over the questions filling it, Cassieus took them over the rolling hills and dirt roads until they reached a small village just two miles from the English border.

"Woah," Ihon yanked the rein when they reached the first stone building at the end of the main road. His eyes jumped from one structure to the other. Nostrils flaring, he nodded.

"He's here," the words tasted like the bitterness in his soul.

Cassieus gave a quick snort and scraped the packed earth beneath his hooves.

Sliding down off of the saddle, his feet barely making a sound in his highland moccasin boots, Ihon took the reins and led them forward. Sniffing the air, he found the origin of the scent to be inside a two-story building in the middle of town.

Must be the Inn, he thought. That son of Belial figured he could hole up here for the night before leaving the country. He won't leave Scotland, unless in a corpse wagon.

Tying the reins to the hitching post in front of the Inn, Ihon inched over to a window. Peering inside, he made out the contents of the room.

It appeared to be a gathering room where people could relax or mingle with the locals.

Doors leading to the back of the building told the stalker the sleeping chambers were in the back.

Tip-toeing around the structure, Ihon noticed one of the windows in the back was hanging wide open. He crept through the shadows toward it and peeked over the ledge.

His nostrils widened.

The scent was rampant inside the room.

He'd found him. The hunter had discovered his wife's murderer. Now, the monster would pay.

The stench was horrible, sending tendrils of disgust into Ihon's gut while he crawled in through the window.

Perhaps I should change into that beast, he wondered. Sounds like a good idea, add a bit more terror into this murderer before he meets his Maker.

With that, Ihon shoved his kilt off and knelt down. His knuckles touching the wood floor of the bedchamber, he shut his eyes and grimaced. In seconds, the midnight fur covered his entire frame which was now thrice its size. The shift, though twisting and realigning bones and muscles, did not hurt.

The only sound was the quick growl that bellowed in the creature's barrel chest.

Still have no idea what under the sun and moon I am, Ihon glanced down at the long claws extending from the tips of his fingers. But who better to bring swift vengeance to a monster than a monster?

His teeth bared, the beast crept through the shadows. Pitch-coloured fur blending in with the darkness around him, he paused. The reek of unclean flesh caused his coarse snout to wrinkle.

Eyes, the colour of smoldering darkness, glared at the hump lying beneath the animal skin blanket.

An early morning breeze whispered through the window. It brushed the nose of the beast while he inched his way to the foot of the large oaken bed. The wind did not seem to understand the depth of the present situation, playing with his large wolf-like ears while they flattened against his enormous head.

A sudden snort interrupted the quiet night.

Ihon froze, rearing up on his hind legs—though he looked like a hulking wolf, his beast form did retain the humanoid postures. The tone of those back leg muscles revealed a strength that was superhuman. This power rippled throughout the entire body—a force no normal human being could ever hope to harness.

"I was expecting you," the shape beneath the blanket growled.

A hand pulled aside the covers to reveal a grinning face half-covered in a raven-black beard.

"Smelled you coming from miles away."

Cutting into a snarl, Ihon lowered his head. Glaring at the man in the bed through his thick eyebrows, he growled.

"Then you know I am here for only one thing."

Swinging his legs over the side of the bed, the man held

his plastered grin while keeping eye contact with the monster.

Ihon flexed his fingers, baring his claws, while his fangs gnashed the air.

The man stood to his feet, the grin turned eerie as it gripped his face.

Another growl started to bellow in Ihon's chest when it was strangled.

His large eyes widening, Ihon watched in shock as the murderer's naked body started to ripple and contort.

Joints twisting, skin rolling like liquid, the hunted villain's body grew. Skin seeming to rip, long silver hair, peppered with brown, drenched the naked figure.

In under a minute, Ihon blanched at the creature now mirroring his stance — as well as his size and appearance.

Except for the coat colour and a few miniscule facial differences — the beasts looked the same.

I'm not alone? Ihon's mind raced.

ere Ihon was, standing in front of a second monster, unable to believe what he saw.

Standing erect, the creature opened his sinewy arms in fighting stance. His brown fur had silvered, revealing his age to be much older than Ihon. But his size and overall wolf-like shape reflected Ihon's.

Ihon felt the wolf-like ears on his own head flatten while his lips curled, baring his fangs.

He'd thought himself the only monster. Was this all a nightmare? Could this all have been conjured up by the wack on his head? Maybe he was still unconscious back at home? Or was he really witnessing something supernatural? Were they the only two or were there any others?

So many questions, no time at all.

Should he execute his vengeance? Maybe he could allow the murderer to live for a little while, enabling himself to extract the answers to all these questions.

Ihon's claws stretched then retracted then stretched again while he paced the floor, dark brown eyes glinting.

His opponent studied him, the large wolf head swiveling back and forth with every step.

"It's almost unbearable," the creature revealed a set of edged fangs. "Isn't it?" His grin sent Ihon's stomach in a bind.

Refusing to give in and speak, Ihon thought of his wife. He could still see her bloodied body in his mind's eye.

"Yes," the villain snickered, a cross between a snarl and a hiss. "The choice between punishing me for your wife's murder or demanding answers for the questions storming your brain."

Ihon stepped sideways to his right, his long tongue running along the tops of his fangs.

"Of course," the villain growled. "There is a third decision."

"You could just die," Ihon spat out.

"You first, it was your life I meant to take."

Ihon caught sight of the quick change in his enemy's prance. Instinctive reflexes in high gear, he sidestepped.

The fur-coated hulk rammed past him and barreled into the floor, splintering the oaken panels.

In the same movement, Ihon jumped on his back and lashed out with his taloned hands, ripping into the fur, tearing the long hair beneath.

"What are you?" Ihon snarled, slicing his claws through the thick coat, trying to find skin in order to lacerate his opponent. "Why did you kill her?"

The murderer lunged to his right, knocking his attacker off his back. In a fluid movement, he spun around and leaped to his feet. Facing Ihon, he hissed.

"First," his voice thick. "I am Wolf-Born as you are. Second, I was sent to kill you, becase of your betrayal of the Knights Templar — your wife happened to be a part of the bargain because she was there."

Ihon's eyes widened, threatening to match the moon. He could feel his heart ramping up the beats, adrenaline dumping into his system.

"I knew they would," he muttered, his voice as soft as thunder. "I just didn't think they'd harm her. Not very knightly. But because I'm like you, I didn't die."

His eyes were flashing now, narrowing into slits of fury.

"What is a Wolf-Born?" He demanded, claws scraping the wood beneath his toes.

The desire to end this abomination ravaged his soul.

"You don't know?" The beast tilted his head. Claws still bared and ready, he shifted his weight. With a shrug, he continued, "The Wolf-Born are a separate Race. We come from humanity but we're not human. Our kind wonder the Earth since the first was born nearly three thousand years ago."

"You mean," Ihon's blurted, unable to believe his ears, his skin crawling. "There are more of us?"

"Yes," the monster growled. "We cannot be killed like a human. Such as your wife, she was not of our Race — had you known, you could have changed her."

"How?"

The villain licked his chops, he seemed to be growing bored.

"In order to be a Wolf-Born, you must either be born to two parents of our Race or you could drink our blood. One drop is enough to bring the Change."

Ihon gaped.

The room was spinning around him.

He could barely breathe, everything was spiraling out of control inside his mind, sending him reeling. He let his guard down.

Finding his chance, the foe snarled and flew across the floor. Tackling Ihon with all his massive frame, he shoved him to the floor, cracking four planks under their weight.

Attempting to block his attacker's blows, Ihon held his arms in front of his face. He gritted through the pain, feeling something warm and sticky dripping over his furry arms. He managed to lash out and felt his claws make contact with the monster's muzzle.

Both creatures bellowed, a death match erupting in the bedchamber.

The bed snapped in two when both bodies plunged on top of it. Splinters and debris were thrown around the room while the two rolled and twisted between each other's punches and slices.

Ihon had never felt so charged, so full of power, swiping his hands and feet through the air.

Animal instinct took over, he pummeled his opponent.

Blood oozed from several wounds all over his body, though they quickly healed.

Lunging at his enemy, Ihon let out an otherworldly roar. Heightened sense of hearing, he noted a commotion now stirring outside the bedchamber's door. He had to end this fast before innocent casualties accumulated.

His claws latched onto the murderer's throat.

Baring his teeth, Ihon went in for the throat.

But with lightning-fast reflexes, the beast beneath gave one quick and powerful kick up between Ihon's legs.

Ihon grimaced as bolts of hot pain sizzled up from his groin into the pit of his stomach.

In beast form, that area was safely hidden and padded but enough force would cause anyone discomfort.

Attempting to regain his composure, Ihon allowed his grip to slacken.

This was exactly what his opponent was hoping for. With one flip, he was on top of Ihon, his powerful arms wrapped around Ihon's throat.

Stars danced in front of Ihon's eyes as he gagged.

He tried to swipe his attacker's arms away.

So this is how I'm going to die, he mused. At least I'll be with Joanna and the children soon.

Attempting to reach around for the killer's throat, he managed to yank a couple tuffs of hair and fur, but that didn't dislodge the oxygen-stifling choke hold.

Then it hit him.

Ihon stopped fighting. Allowing himself to dip into the

blackness of unconsciousness, he let go. Holding on just enough to not succomb all the way, he found it a bit of a struggle.

I just might die here, he thought. Doesn't matter anymore. I don't think.

He didn't care either way now.

If he lived, he would avenge his wife's murder. If he died, he could be with her, Calab, and Susan. What a wondrous thought.

Peace started to caress his heart.

A smile cut across his gasping mouth.

But then, what about justice? The thought raced across his darkening brain.

Justice was something his soul cried for.

ven a dying body can be animated, if there is enough determination.

Ihon reached up with his right hand over his head for the villain's face.

Talons slicing a bloody gash into the skin, his hand found the lips before slipping through between the fangs. They imbedded themselves into the long tongue. At the same time, the thumb dug its own claw into the underside of the jaw.

The hold loosened around his throat while Ihon's attacker tried to swat his grip away.

Breaking through the hold, Ihon spun around with lightning speed to face the spitting Wolf-Born assassin. Without hesitance, he buried his claws into the attacker's eyes. Feeling instinct take over, Ihon ripped the head backward before sinking his fangs into the thick neck muscles. Shredding the bulging red meat, he found the jugular vein and tore it out of the throat. Black blood dripped down his bottom lip off his fangs, Ihon reared back, allowing the limp body to fall to the floor in a heap.

Bile burned the back of his throat.

Dark eyes glaring at the crumbled monster, he reeled. Emotions tore like a hurricane at his wearied body. The rush from the past hour was spent and he dropped on his haunches. All he could do was sit there, head swaying.

His mind looked back over the past week. Everything that happened, bringing him down to this.

Now what am I supposed to do? His brain screamed. Joanna is avenged, but I'm still alone with this monstrous body.

He wondered if these answers would ever be answered.

Could that corpse lying two feet in front of him be the only being on this Earth who could answer them?

Something moved, Ihon gave a startled grunt and leaned forward.

The flesh beneath the fur was decomposing.

That was fast, Ihon remarked to himself.

The long hair and fur shifted into whisps of ghost-like tendrils, disintegrating into nothingness.

By the time it was all dissolved, the skin had shriveled into something that looked like melting clay.

Ihon could not take his eyes off of the scene until the very skeleton had melted into the wooden floor beneath it.

It was then he noticed a silver wrist-band lying in the vanished puddle. Picking it up, he studied it in the darkness. Night vision was something he'd always possessed, never had it dawned on him this wasn't something all humans shared.

The emblem etched into the silver was a cross of the Templar Knights, complete with a skull and crossbones hovering over it.

Ihon stood to his feet, clutching the band in his hand. His eyes surveyed the room once before he trudged over to the window and slipped outside into the cold night air.

His padded feet made barely a sound when he landed.

Better not be seen like this, he decided. Concentrating his senses, he growled and shut his eyes.

His neck arched, sending his face toward the sky and letting loose a gasp. The ripples across his skin, sent a shiver down his spine. In moments, the coat of fur was gone and he was back in his human physique.

It wasn't painful at all, in fact the Change felt good.

Although, being in beast form felt better. It was his natural self he realised. Human form was all right, he could still use most his senses and strength, but being free of human restraints was another thing.

Cassieus gave a soft snort, happy to see his master again, while Ihon slipped the wristband into one of the saddlebags.

Pulling a set of clothes out of another bag, he donned a pair of breeches and saffron shirt before pulling a black cloak over his frame. At the sound of voices coming from just inside the Inn's front door, he reached back and covered his head with the hood, its shadows inside blanketing most of his face.

"Did ye hear that ruckus in the back?"

The front door swung open, creaking on its hinges.

A man with a torso the size of a barrel stepped through. He was gripping the handle to a small burning lamp.

Hanging on his arm was a middle-aged woman, obviously his wife. She peered into the night, eyes searching.

When they rested on Ihon's figure, dressed in the black cloak, now seated in his saddle atop his midnight-coloured battle steed, they grew near the size of saucers.

She patted the Innkeeper on his shoulder and pointed at the strange apparition.

The man blanched when he noticed the phantom. His eyes revealed the question screaming in his brain.

Were they being haunted by some ethereal spirit? Had that noise from the back room been caused by this being? Was it Death himself coming for his dues?

"Get back inside, dear," he muttered to his wife, nearly tripping over the doorstep while shoving her back. He almost dropped the lamp before slamming the door behind him.

"I think we scared them, Cassieus," Ihon smirked beneath the cowl.

The horse nodded his head but made no sound. He was tired.

"Yeah," Ihon nodded back. "I'm tired too, old boy. Let's go find us a place to settle down outside of town."

Without any encouragement, the steed trudged back out beyond the buildings. His hooves clomping in the dirt,

Cassieus found a small knoll overlooking the village. He paused, waiting to be dismounted.

Ihon dropped to the earth and went about unsaddling the mount. Setting it on the ground, he sat down and leaned back against it. Staring up at the stars, he let his thoughts rampage about again.

The storm brewed dark inside his mind.

He needed to let it out or he felt he might explode. The urge to run grew stronger by the second.

Standing to his feet, he undid the clasp that held his cloak and tossed it to the ground. Stashing the rest of his clothes with it, he tip-toed down the incline, not wanting to awaken his horse. Closing his eyes, he lowered his head, bringing on the transformation.

Like a mighty whirlwind, the power inside broke and crashed inside him, a force pouring into his body.

Raven black fur erupted again, starting from his shoulders down his front, waving out across his appendages.

While his arms and legs bulged, his head tensed before growing larger with the rest of his body, something rumbled in the bottom of his stomach. It ached to climb up his throat.

Swallowing hard, Ihon felt it ascend to the back of his maw. Before he knew it, his head jerked back to look up at the night sky.

A howl, loud and lonely, broke across his tongue and reached for the stars.

The Change complete, Ihon sniffed the air.

Smelling of salt water, it let him know the ocean was within his ten mile diameter. He realised that was the extent of his sense of smell.

Powerful feet kicked the air before pounding the earth when he tore down the valley between two hills.

Dark eyes flashing, he charged across the grassy rolls, senses heightened while his tongue lolled against his fangs.

You are free, he smiled. He was certain his thoughts were racing as fast as the black blood he knew was coursing through his veins.

Pushing himself, he headed back to town, the speed of his legs sent a rush to his brain. He'd never run so fast in his life before.

The buildings whipped by while he dashed down the road, within seconds they were miles behind him.

The wind roared over his thick coat with a rejuvinating force, filling his powerful lungs while he broke across the English countryside, zipping through a nearby forest.

A deep laugh rumbled in his chest, nearly startling him, his head spinning with elation.

Breathing deeply, he noticed a small cliff lay beyond another hill he was crossing. He calmed his nerves while letting the adrenaline pump more energy into his veins. With another howl, he leaped over the edge, landing fourteen feet ahead on an opposing hill.

The sky seemed closer up here and its billions of sparkling stars caught Ihon's attention.

The beast lurched to a stop, clawed feet tearing at the grass, sending clumps of dirt in the air. Staring up at the glorious beauty of the universe, the Wolf-Born was mes-merised, his fangs gleaming in the moonlight.

The moon was beckoning to him, sending a finger of yearning into his core.

This yearning turned into a rumble deep in his chest. It grew in intensity until he could not hold it in.

The howl that escape his muzzle rippled over the rolling hills. It echoed across the nearby forest all the way to a lonely farmer's cottage where the occupant stirred in dreamless sleep, his old heart touched by the cry of what he thought was a wolf.

Moments passed while Ihon took in the night breeze that rustled his fur, causing it to shimmer like dark waves in the moonlight. Eyes dropping to the ocean horizon in the distance, he could see the red hues of the sun reaching for morning.

I wonder if Cassieus has had a good night sleep yet, he wondered. Probably a good idea to head back in a minute.

His nose twitched.

His sense of smell let him know there was a herd of does munching on their predawn breakfast just twenty yards from his position.

Stomach growling, he realised he hadn't eaten since yesterday and the beast wouldn't be happy if he went any longer without food.

First I'll have breakfast, he told himself. He crouched down and slinked below the hill.

While he approched his prey, his nose caught a whiff of something else.

Wrinkling his forehead, the Wolf-Born breathed in the scent.

It tasted familiar yet not like anything he'd smelled.

Shrugging it off at another gurgle from his gut, he focused his attention on the upcoming meal. Little did he know of the dark silver eyes watching him from behind a group of trees almost a mile away.

9

Reaching over to the other side of the bed, Ihon's hand found an empty sheet.

Air shot between his lips when he sat upright with a start. Ihon stared at his hand now clutching the bedspread at his side. For a moment, his mind foggy, he couldn't think of why Joanna wasn't lying there.

She normally waits till I'm awake before heading into the kitchen to make breakfast while I feed the animals.

Oh, that's right.

His brow furrowed and he slumped back on his pillow.

His chest burned.

I miss you, my love, his mind called out. *But, I did accomplish what I set out for. You have been avenged. Now if only I knew why the Templar Knights would go to such great lengths to have me killed. I was but a member for less than a year.*

His mind trudged through the past, reluctant to think of the war.

He hated war.

One thing he hated more than war was people who prowled on the weak. This is the reason he'd joined the Second Crusade. From what his mother had told him growing up, the First was the same. It was a retaliation for four hundred years of invasion and slaughter.

There comes a time when the sons of Belial mess with the wrong Christians, she had made the remark.

Ihon's mouth teased him with a smile. Though she'd passed away before he turned fifteen, Ihon always felt close to his mother. Sometimes he wished he knew his father, but at times, he knew the two of them were looking down from Heaven watching their son.

"Mother," he looked to the ceiling. "Did you know I was a Wolf-Born? Whatever that may be."

A morning breeze whistled in between the closed window panels.

His eyes wrenching to the window, he stared at it, his mind miles and years away.

"You did tell me several times that you had a secret to share with me when you thought me ready. Could this be the secret?"

His thoughts turned to the night before. After the execution and the run, he'd returned to grab Cassieus and the two of them walked twenty miles northward, stopping at another village to spend the night in an Inn.

But it was the murderer's words that now gripped his core.

"In order to be a Wolf-Born, you must either be born to two parents of our Race or you could drink our blood. One drop is enough to bring the Change."

I have never drank a single drop of my mother's or my father's blood—at least, I don't remember tasting such a thing.

The two brows above his brown eyes lifted ever so slowly as the thought dawned on his consciousness.

Could it be? He wondered, his breaths jumping speed levels. What if that is what the secret was? Both my parents were Wolf-Born. Why would they keep such a thing from me?

If only both—or at least, one—of his parents were still alive. They could answer the army of questions invading his brain.

Jumping to his feet, Ihon shook himself. Reining in the racing sensation pulsing through his veins, he rubbed the bridge of his nose with his index finger and thumb. Shuffling about the room, he reached for his kilt draped over a wooden chair, the only piece of furniture in the room besides the bed.

It was then that he noticed it.

Freezing in midstep, he studied the slip of deerskin paper lying on the floor at the foot of the cherry-wood door.

Someone must have slipped it under before Ihon awoke.

Sniffing the air, he didn't smell anyone nearby, except for the Innkeeper whose room was on the second floor just above this one. Beside that, his nose told him there were no other occupants in this building.

The deerskin was shaved of its hair, making room for the charcoal scribblings noticeable across its breadth.

Sweeping his hand down, Ihon picked the parchment up and tossed it over in his hands. Befuddled, he turned it back over and started reading the black-coloured words.

At first, the language of the text appeared to be a mixture of Scots Gaelic, Latin, and even Greek — then it dawned on the reader, it was its own species.

What shocked Ihon was the fact he could read it.

"You are who you are," it began. The handwriting was clipped, apparently the writer did not want to waste time. "You can read this because of who you are. From what I've witnessed, you only recently discovered your true self and, most likely, have a million questions. Meet me in the stable where your horse resides. I will bring these answers."

That was all. The period seemed to be a bit emphatic for a simple sentence.

Ihon reread the paragraph. Then, his mind still trying to wrap itself around this moment, he read it a third time. Finding the chair with his left hand, he lowered himself into it. Running his hand through his thick beard, he studied the parchment, flipping it over then over again in his right hand.

This was a strange twist of events. Could it be that someone was sending him the answers? Was God truly interested in his measley — though preternatural — life? Or was this another Templar Knight sent to assassinate him?

Realising he was holding his breath, Ihon sat up and inhaled with a brisk start.

Were all the Templar Knights Wolf-Born? Is that why they'd invited him to join so many years ago? But then, there had been a distinct smell about the former assassin. His gut told him it had something to do with his kind—he did not recall ever tasting that odour while walking among the ranks of the Knights.

Then again, he was the same type of beast and he did not notice a smilar scent arising from his own pores.

Eyes dropping to the piece of skin one more time, he pursed his lips.

I guess there's only one way to find out. If this is another threat, it won't last long. If not, I'll finally have some answers. All I have to do is head over right now.

His stomach growled.

Tossing the note on his bed, he stood up and hurrieldy draped the kilt about his frame, attaching it together with the broch and belt. Strapping his claymore—which was waiting next to the bed—to his back. He surveyed the room for a moment, taking in its lacklustre arrangement.

He could hear the neighing and snorting coming from the stables, informing him the horses were waking up and ready for breakfast themselves.

The door creaked when he yanked it open.

His face turned from side to side while he made his way across the street—studying passersby as they crossed the village on their way to the market or mill, wherever their daily errands took them. Slipping inside the stable, he paused after shutting the door behind himself.

Ears perked, he scrutinized the large room with its lined stalls.

Among the horse heads peeking out in all their various colours, Cassieus turned his head to look at his master. With a brief greeting by nodding his head, the old horse stuffed his nose in a leather bag hanging on the doorpost, sounds of crunching oats emanated from the bag.

"My friend," Ihon approached the stall. "Has anyone strange been in here? I'm looking for a stranger—someone left a note under my door a few minutes ago, telling me to meet here."

Ihon's nostrils flared—he could smell that familiar scent, only this one did not seem like evil incarnate. In fact, it reminded him of his own odour.

Strange, he thought.

"You talk to your horse as if he were a person," a deep voice spoke up in Scots Gaelic.

"Aye," Ihon turned to face the shadow that now stood filling the open doorway of the next stall over. "It's because he is."

"Did he carry you into battle during the last Crusade?" The silhouette held his stance, keeping every part of his physical features in darkness.

Ihon raised an eyebrow.

Why would this stranger want to know whether his steed was a Crusade veteran like himself? Why did the individual remain in the shadows?

"Why don't you step into the light of that lamp yonder,

friend?" He asked, waving his right hand in the general direction of a flickering candle in a clay pot.

"Perhaps I love the shade," Ihon could hear the smile cutting the stranger's lips.

Right hand now moving behind his back, checking the sheath, making sure he had the claymore waiting, Ihon gazed at the stranger.

It was then that the figure took two steps forward, allowing the light from the lamp and the midday sun outside to flood his face.

Wearing a blue tunic wrapped at the waist with a leather belt, the man stood there with a warm smile. Though his figure was draped with a leather breastplate and sheath at his waist carrying a two foot long dirk, he looked cordial.

Sniffing the breeze again, Ihon took in the scent, his eyes penetrating the mysterious man.

"By now," the man returned the gaze with two steel gray eyes. "I hope you've realised we share the same scent and that assassin you dispatched was similar, only with the blot of the curse on it."

"Curse?" Ihon could only muster one word, his left eyebrow lifting into a furrowed brow.

"Yes," the man shifted onto his right foot, seeming relaxed. "He was what our kind call a Rogue."

"Our kind?" Ihon repeated those two words, his head was beginning to reel, the world felt like it decided to spin a bit faster. "So he wasn't lying? We are an actual Race?"

"Yes, the Wolf-Born Race," the man nodded, his smile spreading. "How old are you?"

"I just turned fifty years, but what does that matter?"

"I am shocked you've made it this far not knowing what you are," his voice was a bit deeper than Ihon's. "Did your parents never tell you? I'm horrified any parent would conceal such a secret from their offspring."

"My father died in a war before I was old enough to know him. My mother died before I became a man through some illness."

"Most likely poisoned," the stranger rubbed the stubble on his chin with his left hand. "Wolf-Born's don't catch illnesses."

Ihon blanched. The jolt in his arms tingled like electricity.

"Forgive me," the man waved his hand in front of him. "My name is Ranvir. I've been following you since I noticed your rampage last night. I knew, from the way you ran, it was your first time coming to know your true self. I had to meet you. I have the answers to most of your questions, if you're willing to ask."

Studying Ranvir's face, Ihon met his gaze. Trying to decipher the true intent behind those eyes, something in his gut told him there was nothing to be concerned over. This Ranvir truly did wish to answer his million questions.

"Why do you think my mother was poisoned? Or for that matter, a Wolf-Born?"

"Because the only way one can be of the Race, he must be born to two parents of the blood of Tiras. You do not carry the scent of the cursed, therefore not a Rogue as the assassin you executed yesterday, and thus you could not have been changed by drinking the blood of one."

"So just by drinking a Wolf-Born's blood, you can become one but are automatically cursed? Why?"

"That is how God Almighty outlined it in His law."

"Law? You mean the Holy Script? The ones the Apostles handed down to the Church fathers?"

"No," Ranvir shook his head. "I speak of a separate Law. It is for our kind and ours alone. It was given to the first Supreme Council of the Wolf-Born Race almost three thousand years ago. We call it the Ancient Creed. This is why sometimes our people are referred to as the People of the Creed."

"Wait," Ihon had to sit down, the room was spinning too fast for him now. Gripping the post of Cassieus's stall, he slumped onto a wooden stool.

"Forgive me," Ranvir knelt down to reach eye level with the newbie. He then adjusted his dirk and plopped down on the barn's hay-strewn, dirt floor. "Why don't I start at the beginning?"

Ihon rubbed the edges of his temples before meeting Ranvir's gaze. He then gave a nod.

"You remember Noah?"

"I've heard of him," Ihon pursed his lips. "The father of the new human race after the old was destroyed by the Great Flood?"

"Yes, the one and only," Ranvir grinned. "Noah had

three sons. Japheth, Shem, and Ham. Japheth went on to have seven sons, the youngest was called Tiras. Tiras lived around the time of the ancient empires—such as the Egyptian dynasties, they were, in fact, going through their Golden Age. Tiras was given the Wolf gift by the Almighty when he reached the age of three hundred years, the night he lost his first wife. After that, most do not know what happened to him. All we know, he traveled the world, visiting the nations, tribes, and cultures of the earth during its early days."

"Sounds like most ancient myths," Ihon butted in. He did not know what to believe at the moment.

"It is not a myth, this is a true account," Ranvir gave a look that said he did not wish for any funny business. "Tiras was guided by the Almighty to Egypt where he met the Princess, Kissa. He gave her the Gift, she became his wife, and they became the Father and Mother of the Wolf-Born Race."

"Amazing story," Ihon nodded. "But how does it relate to me?"

"They had many children. Who was your father?"

"His name was Justin, he came from Rome many years ago."

It was Ranvir's turn to blanche. He gaped up at Ihon's face as if he were meeting some sort of high-class official.

"Justin of Rome? You are the son of Justin of Rome?"

"Umm," Ihon raised his right eyebrow. "I believe so, my Mother told me that."

"Who was your mother? Wait," Ranvir raised a hand to stop the forthcoming reply. "Let me guess. Would I be wrong if I ascertained her name was Ariel McFaye?"

Eyes growing the size of saucers, Ihon stared at the stranger. That was, in fact, his mother's name—how in the worlds did this odd stranger know that?

"Yes?" Ranvir's mouth was widening in such a grin Ihon was sure its corners would touch the ears in a matter of seconds.

Finally forcing his head to bob up and down in the affirmative, Ihon could not find the words to say.

"I knew it," Ranvir jumped to his feet. "I knew Justin of Rome had offspring. My father was good friends with him, he told me of the time during the Second Great War after the Second Migration, when Justin met a woman by the name of Ariel McFaye. She was on a pilgrimage from Scotland. They fell in love and Justin disappeared. My father always surmised they'd left for Scotland."

"Yes, yes," Ihon nodded. "Mother always said they'd lived in Rome for a couple months before moving here to the Highlands where she had me. But what are you talking about with the 'second great war' and the 'second migration'?"

Ranvir twisted around on the floor, swinging his legs up under himself Indian-style.

"The Second Migration is what we give to the period of time when more than half of our people, including the Supreme Council, moved to the Scottish Highlands. You see, we'd originally established our own city somewhere in the mountains of Anatolia, around the kingdom of Turkey."

"We have our own city?" Ihon interrupted the ecstatic teacher.

Raising a hand for silence, Ranvir continued.

"We moved the city to Rome after a few of our memebers helped build it. In fact, our Race has been responsible for the founding of many ancient cities, Rome, Constantinople, even Troy. But shortly after Rome became a strong city, the Supreme Council decided to move there, that was the First Migration. The Second was to Sanguiatro, hidden deep in the Highlands of Scotland."

"Sanguiatro?" Ihon repeated the name. The clip of the word stirred his core—as if it was a long lost home.

"Yes," Ranvir nodded. He then reached out and patted Ihon on the shoulder. "You should come with me. I can show you our wondrous city. You can meet the Council and they can answer your questions better than I."

"But you seem to be doing a good job so far? It may be overwhelming for me at the moment—it's a lot to take in—but, with time, I can process it."

"Did I mention we have the largest library in the world, since Alexandria?"

Jumping to his feet, Ihon dusted himself off.

"Why didn't you say that in the first place? Let's go!" He turned to unlatch the stall where his horse waited.

Cassieus could sense the excitement sizzling the air. He stamped the ground.

"It is only two days ride from here," Ranvir sashayed over to a second stall and opened it. He reached in and led a chestnut mare out.

"That yours?" Ihon peered over his shoulder while he strapped on the saddle over his black steed.

"Of course," Ranvir winked at him before tossing a saddle onto the snorting mare.

Ihon shrugged before finishing up the preparation for the ride. Swinging his leg up and over, he glanced at his new companion.

"Are all Peoples of the Creed as slow as you in saddling a horse?"

"Well," Ranvir muttered through gritted teeth. "We don't normally ride horses, our own legs take us places a lot faster."

Ihon nodded, he didn't have a reply. Based on his experience last night, he could believe it. A smiled teased the corners of his mouth when the memory of wind racing over his fur came to mind.

"All right," Ranvir jumped into the saddle. Adjusting his weight, he looked ready to topple off. It had been awhile since he'd ridden a horse, but the look on his face showed he would not admit this to anyone.

Ihon grinned — not knowing whether to tease the man or not. He nudged Cassieus forward instead.

The barn door opened just then.

"Where do you two think you're going?" A man, dressed in peasant's garb, stood defiantly in between the large doors. He gripped the door with his left hand, a pitchfork clutched in the other.

10

A wave of goose bumps rose on the back of Ihon's neck. He stared at the man now glaring at them.

"You think you can leave without making payment?" The peasant demanded.

Letting out a breath, Ihon could not help but smile. He nodded, raising his hands in the air.

"Forgive us, Sir," he replied. "We forgot." With that he rummaged through his saddle-bag and found a few silver coins. Leaning over, he handed them to the open palm of the stable-keeper.

"I better receive my just due," the man almost yanked the coins from Ihon's outstretched hand. Everyhing about him looked sour, his tunic, his face, the sneer beneath his beard.

"As you have," Ihon nodded, his own smile dissipating. With that, he prodded his mount out the open doors.

Ranvir followed. When he passed, he tossed a couple coins over his shoulder and chuckled when he glanced that way to see the peasant scrambling to the hay-covered floor.

"You're cruel," Ihon lifted an eyebrow.

Both riders trudged down the muddy road, exiting the village.

"I don't like greedy people," Ranvir shrugged.

"Agreed," Ihon nodded.

After that, silence joined the traveling companions.

Three seagulls cried overhead, searching for a mid-afternoon meal before locating a place to rest for the evening. This was joined by the rustle of leaves in the pines nearby.

Cassieus slowed a bit, distracted by a clump of heather.

Ranvir's mare plodded onward.

Ihon nudged the old stallion forward, his eyes turning to Ranvir's figure.

"How old are you?" He found himself asking. Not sure why, but he guessed it was his mind trying to keep things interesting on this trip.

"I'll be forty-three two days after St. Valentine's Day."

So several years younger than me, Ihon nodded. I thought so. No wonder he was so shocked I knew nothing of our Race.

The forest that surrounded a glen in its natural embrace grew in size. Its pines, oaks, and other species of trees gave shade to any passerby.

The glen stretched out for about a mile before shifting into rolling hills.

The Lowlands were favoured by most Scots, but Ihon had always found the Highlands much more inviting. Perhaps it was simply his upbringing, but he'd always thrilled over their dark mysteries.

"Who was your father, Ranvir?" He piped up. One hand gripping the reins, the other scratching his chin, stroking the beard. How he wished he could trim the thing.

Ranvir was quiet, his glinting eyes stared out at a lake they were nearing.

The dark green waters reached for the forest, splitting it in two before disappearing behind a grassy knoll.

Their horses plodding through the mud, skirting the lake, were peeved, their disgruntled snorts informing their riders they did not appreciate the sucking scum beneath their hooves.

"My father was Brian Caiton," Ranvir finally replied. "They were good friends, our fathers. They remained with their families in Rome until the end of the Second Migration when they finally moved up here. Enlisting into the forces when the Second Great War began, they served together. My father was Justin Iraes's second-in-command. That is Justin's sword you carry, right?"

Ihon reached over his shoulder to run his finger along the handle of the old claymore. He nodded.

"The symbol etched into its hilt," Ranvir continued. "Let me guess, you've thought it to be a family crest of some sort?"

"Yes," Ihon gave a half-nod, he felt like his world was beginning to shatter, everything he thought he knew was, apparently, not true.

Not true at all, he shivered. He wondered why his mother had kept this a secret.

"It isn't," Ranvir interrupted his thoughts. He reached under his tunic and pulled out a silver pendant attached to a small chain around his thick neck. Pointing to the carved crest on its face, he explained the object. "This is actually an insignia, letting the rest of the Creed Army know what rank you are."

"Seriously?" Ihon held Cassieus at the same pace as his companion's chestnut mount. He leaned toward Ranvir to try to catch a better view of the etching.

Looking similar to the crest on his father's Claymore, the wolf's head set against a full moon.

"This is the mark of a Lesser Officer of the Order of the Creed. That's my rank." Ranvir informed. He then pointed to Ihon's sword as he continued. "That is the rank insignia of a Higher Officer of the Order of the Creed, your father was one."

"The Order of the Creed is what you call our people's Army?"

"Yes," Ranvir nodded, his eyes perusing the mountains now jutting up around them.

It would be dusk soon, near time they should find a place to camp for the night.

"Though these ranks are mostly just for times of war. Which, the Second Great War ended a few years after you were born, if I remember correctly, six years after I was born."

Ihon felt like he was now devouring these revelations—yes, his world was still shattered, more like blown up, but he found this to be fascinating. He was hungry for more.

"Are you the only Lesser Officer?"

"No," his companion shook his head with a chuckle. He pointed over to a short knoll that looked as if it had been carved into the side of a rocky mountain by the finger of God Almighty. "There are twenty-four of us."

Ihon nodded. He nudged his stallion to the right, following the tromping mare.

"Your father was a Higher Officer of the Order, since his death, there are only nine of those. We are all given special missions by the Supreme Council during the intermissions between the wars. Although, even when our Race isn't having a war, we seem to get our fill of mankind's wars."

"This is true," Ihon's mind went back to the time he served in the Middle East. He then spoke up as the two horses arrived at the knoll and paused.

"And the Roman numerals etched into my crest, what do those stand for?"

"They are the year of the founding of the Supreme Council."

"Seventeen-hundred-and-seventeen?" Ihon raised an eyebrow. "You mean, all those years before the time of Christ's birth?"

"Aye, that time," Ranvir grinned. He swung his leg over his saddle and jumped to the ground with a cushioned thud. Shifting the dirk sheath, he went about gathering sticks for a fire.

Ihon joined in, processing this information, his eyebrows furrowed. Leaning over, he picked a rock the size of his fist then stepped over to another. Gathering several under his arm, he then moved to the centre of the knoll and laid them in a circular pattern.

"My father was on leave for a month in Rome, he spent this time with my mother," Ranvir continued his story while he set the branches and logs in the middle of the stone circle. "This was when I was conceived. Shortly after he returned to your father's command here in the Highlands, they were both slain in the last battle, giving us the final victory of the Second Great War."

"You keep speaking of these Great Wars," Ihon started rubbing two firm sticks together. In seconds, he watched as a wisp of smoke began spiraling upward, how he loved the scent of burning pine.

"Yes, there have been two," Ranvir nodded, watching the tiny tongue of flame that sprang from the ground sticks. "There is word that a third may soon begin."

"Who do we fight these wars with?" Ihon leaned back on his haunches to gaze into the face of his traveling companion. "My gut tells me it is not with the humans."

Ranvir chuckled — not that he found anything hilarious, this was more of a bitterness drooling down his bearded chin.

Ihon raised an eyebrow but remained silent, waiting for the answer.

"They are called the Spawn," Ranvir started, speaking the words as if they tasted like poison. "They are sentient undead who love to prey on human beings. But they usually only suck the blood, leaving the bodies behind as completely drained corpses."

Ihon felt a cold shiver climb up his spine. He shook his shoulders and focused his eyes on the fire that was now burning at a steady pace.

Ranvir plopped down and pulled his feet under himself. He grabbed a small stick and started poking the campfire.

"They have the power to convert their prey into their own ranks as well."

"This sounds familiar," Ihon ran his fingers through his beard then brushed a stray lock of hair out of his face. "I heard a couple local tales in a town I passed through down in France on my way home from the Second Crusade. I thought it was just some myth the town clergy came up with to scare the people into church attendance. It was about some demon who only walked around at night, sucking on the necks of anyone who happened to be up that late."

"Sounds like our enemy," Ranvir nodded, his mouth twisted in a not-so-friendly smile.

"And these Spawn," Ihon cleared his throat. "What is their origin? Where did they come from?"

"From the pits of Hell, I believe," his companion growled, tossing the stick onto the pile of burning wood. "Before the Second Great War, I was told by my uncle, Claric, that there were hundreds of thousands of Spawn. They were ruled by, what they called, the Elite Spawn. According to my uncle, there were nine."

Ihon's gut was now twisting into knots. He no longer felt the pangs of hunger.

"Are they still alive?"

Ranvir raised his silver eyes and met Ihon's stare. He then nodded, his jaw clenched.

"The first Elite Spawn was born the same day Tiras, our Father, changed the Mother of our Race. The story goes, this First Spawn was actually her father, the Pharaoh of Egypt at the time. Not much is spoken of him—I think he still walks the earth."

"So," Ihon's eyes were wider than usual. "He's been around for thousands of years?"

Ranvir nodded again.

The ground beneath him seemed to wobble, Ihon leaned forward and rubbed the bridge of his nose between his fingers.

This was a lot to take in.

"What about these Rogues you were speaking of earlier?"

"They too have Elites among their ranks." Ranvir already saw the question coming.

"And what is their origin?"

"Honestly," Ranvir pursed his lips in thought, his eyes showed he was obviously witnessing dark memories in his mind of past battles. "A Rogue is merely one of our Race who rejects and breaks at least one of the tenets of the Ancient Creed—or all of them. Though they basically run alone, without packs, they have a sort of loose heirarchy—whoever is the strongest is an Elite. There used to be eight."

He paused after this last sentence and made sure to catch Ihon's gaze.

"There are seven now," he smirked.

Ihon tilted his head sideways. His face paled as the dawning arose in his mind.

"You mean, the assassin who murdered my wife was an Elite Rogue?"

"Aye," Ranvir grinned. "Before you even knew of our existence, you annihilated one of our worst enemies. You will be hailed as a hero upon reaching Sanguiatro, most likely."

Ihon cleared his throat. He lay back against a tree trunk, certain he wasn't going to get any sleep tonight.

Ranvir chuckled as he too found a comfortable spot to rest on. He shut his eyes and in minutes was snoring away.

Ihon stared up at the stars, his dark eyes glinting in their light.

"Dear God," he breathed. "This is overwhelming—I want to ask why you kept this hidden from me for so long, but I know not to question your timing. Your will be done, Amen."

The night drifted on.

An old owl hooted nearby before going silent when the howl of an alpha wolf cut the air.

Ihon, still unable to sleep, stared off into the distance—from his point of view, he could see for a couple miles between the mountains. His sense of smell told him the pack of Highland wolves were on a hunt nine miles to the west of his perch.

His chest rose in a deep breath.

Something inside tugged at him, like the Beast wanted out.

A smile creased the corners of his mouth as he thought of the hunt he'd taken the last night. How he had savoured the thrill.

While a light slumber overtook him, he promised the Beast there would be more hunts in the near future.

~

When morning came, the two travelers stirred at the sounds of their horses snorting.

Nuzzles to the ground, Cassieus grazed next to the chestnut mare.

Ihon opened his eyes, remaining still for a moment. His mind racing, he thought of the previous night's discussion. Taking a moment to grasp the truth, that this was all still true, he slowly sat up.

"Good morning," Ranvir cracked the peaceful air, he was already up.

Ihon turned and greeted his companion with a nod. He breathed in and immediately found his mouth watering.

Ranvir was finishing up strapping a large rabbit to a stick. He grunted as he set the stick across two large branches that were dug into the earth on opposite sides of the fire.

The smell of roasting meat sent Ihon's gut into a tantrum of growling.

"Sounds like someone is ready for breakfast already,"

Ranvir chuckled. He carved off a leg from the roasting corpse and tossed it to Ihon.

Catching the leg in mid-air, Ihon studied it for three seconds.

Still partly raw, the meat was red with freshness.

Ihon's teeth started to grow, the Beast was starving. He had to concentrate hard to keep from bringing on the Change. Using the partly-grown fangs, he tore into the leg. In less than a minute, he'd gulped the entire thing down.

"When we reach Sanguiatro," Ranvir nodded. "We will be fed a king's meal."

Ihon wiped a drizzle of blood from his mouth with the back of his hand.

"Does this city's population only consist of Wolf-Born?"

"For the most part," his teacher stoked the fire to keep the meat cooking. "There may be two or three humans who live there—but we do try to keep our identity secret from the world. It is a Law. Our Father thought it best that we work in the shadows to protect the children of God."

Ihon nodded, it made sense.

Humans were a fickle Race who feared anything they did not understand.

From his travels, Ihon was used to hearing humans tell stories of monsters, always painting them as evil creatures hell-bent on destroying humanity.

Now, in the case of the Spawn, they were obviously right.

"You look troubled, my friend," Ranvir lifted the roasted rabbit off its spokes and began slicing it in half. He handed one half to Ihon.

Taking the slice, Ihon shrugged.

"Just processing everything I learned from your talk yesterday."

"You don't even know the half of it yet," Ranvir chuckled while he bit into his half of breakfast. "Wait till we get there."

After finishing their meal, the two saddled their horses, doused the campfire, and took off. Following a barely-used trail between the feet of the mountains, the travellers were both quiet for most of the trip.

While his thoughts trudged through the past week's events and revelations, Ihon found himself reaching down his leather vest beneath his kilt for the cold silver that pressed against his chest.

Hanging from its chain, the necklace felt like it belonged inside his grip.

Pulling it out, Ihon studied the gem.

"May I ask what that is, my friend?" Ranvir had noticed this little ordeal. His eyes studied the necklace as if it were a special artifact, he knew it had to be something owned by his new friend's deceased wife.

"It belonged to Joanna," Ihon replied, his mouth almost didn't want to say her name. The pang was still fresh in his heart. "We were visiting a market, near the end of our time of handfastening, when I bought it for her. It was a sort of wedding gift."

Ranvir nodded, his face turned forward, giving his friend a few moments of privacy.

Stashing the necklace back inside his shirt, Ihon cleared his throat and focused on the mountain that lay in front of them.

"How much longer may I ask?"

Ranvir smiled, glancing at his companion. He then raised his right hand and pointed at the mountain.

"She lies beyond that peak."

Ihon raised both eyebrows. His mouth suddenly felt dry. An electric pulse tinged his wrists. This was going to be a moment he would never forget.

In minutes, their mounts climbed the edge of the rocky giant.

Between all the boulders that jutted up from the face of the mountain, Ihon barely managed to make out a lake just beyond.

Then Cassieus let out a whiny, sounding impressed, as the travellers came over the crest of a steep cliff. He froze when he felt his rider go stiff.

Overlooking a wide valley, the mountain was covered on this side by a thick forest. On the opposite side, a second mountain, crescent in shape, branched out, nearly touching its fellow rocky guardian.

Ihon surmised its height to be well over a thousand feet.

But that wasn't what held him stiff with awe.

Below them, sitting next to the lake, stretched out across the valley at the foot of that mountain, was a large town — more like city.

Stuck in the corner that met in the middle of the opposing mountain's crescent shaped arms was a large Keep built of dark grey stones, looking black in the shade of the mountain.

"There she is," Ranvir smiled as if seeing an old friend he hadn't seen in years. "Sanguiatro."

11

Canting his head, Ihon turned to his new friend.

"Dark blood?"

Ranvir smiled, glancing at the questioning face of the new arrival.

"Aye," his smile was almost reaching his ears.

It was obvious he hadn't been home in ages.

"A Wolf-Born's blood is darker than a human's. Surely you've noticed this?"

Ihon raised both eyebrows—everything was coming together. His mind raced back to every single wound he'd ever received in his fifty years of life. He'd always wondered why his blood always appeared darker than everyone else's.

Their mounts strode into the city.

Ihon took in the sights, he realised he was holding his breath. Breathing out then in, he attempted to keep a regular pace.

This was not your regular city in Scotland—in the Highlands for that matter. Nowhere in the rustic northern lands would anyone find such a spectacle. In the Highlands of Scotland, most travellers would see villages made up of shephards, fishermen, farmers — most poor, barely scraping by in their dirt-floor, thatched houses or caves.

In this city, Sanguiatro, Ihon saw no poor man.

Every house was built of fine carpentry and stonemason work, craftmenship with rare equal. The folks wore fine clothing, most appeared to be of the higher class. Even those who were apparently of the middle class seemed to be well off.

They still had the same jobs, from the bray of a nearby flock of sheep. A herd of goats bleated as they passed by the two visitors.

From the crest of a hill that stood at the southside of the city's fringe, Ihon could see the lake beyond the distant buildings.

A few fishing boats caught his eyes.

"Are all Wolf-Born of such high estate?"

Ranvir grinned. He winked at his companion as he replied.

"Aye," his voice a bit low. He glanced at a young woman who was leading the flock of sheep, giving her a nod, before continuing. "Seeing as the average lifespan of our Race is one thousand and one hundred years, it gives each of us plenty of time to hone our crafts. Working together in peace, our People have built such a magnificant example of unity, don't you agree?"

"A thousand and one hundred years?" Ihon blanched. He could barely spit out the words. "We live a thousand

and one hundred years?" Repeating the statement did nothing to asuage the racing of his heart and mind. Certain he would topple from his saddle, thanks to the spinning world around him, he tried to focus on Ranvir.

"That we do," Ranvir's clipped brogue answered him.

Ihon dropped his gaze to Cassieus's ears.

They flicked back and forth, the old stallion was just as awed at these new sights as his master.

Ranvir could sense the turmoil broiling within his new friend's soul. He nodded and clenched his teeth for a moment.

"It is both a blessing and a curse," he agreed to the unspoken question. "You and I are but children compared to many in this city alone."

"How many of our Race are there?" Ihon blirted out.

"In this city alone, I estimate, at least five thousand. But from what I've heard, there is at least ten times that many all over the known world."

A dog yapped at Cassieus's heels. When it realised it wasn't being noticed, the animal took off down the street to find someone else to annoy.

Not wanting to think of what he'd just learned, Ihon changed the subject. His gaze lifting forward up the city street they were on, he realised it was taking them straight up the side of the mountain to where the Keep stood in its dark glory.

"Are we headed there?" He questioned.

Ranvir gave a nod.

"I assume that's where your governing body resides?"

Again, a nod was given by Ihon's companion.

Ihon then dipped his own head a couple times, wondering why his companion had gone silent. But he was too focused on studying the old structure to ask.

Ranvir most likely was realising how much he'd missed the place.

Set at its base was a built in coutryard, guarded by protruding walls made of the same black brick. At the central front, was a gate made from monolithic iron bars pointing heavenward, fashioned like gigantic spears.

Reaching the gate, both riders came to a halt.

Two hulking sentries stood on either side of the gate. Dressed in full body armour and carrying their own array of weapons, they peered down their noses at the visitors.

Ihon watched as the one on the right raised an eyebrow.

Obviously he'd recognised Ranvir.

With a curt nod, he turned, along with his partner, and unhitched the padlock before dragging the gate open.

Ranvir returned the bow of his chin and nudged his mare forward.

Ihon followed through the open gates.

Inside, the courtyard was mostly furbished with a marble platform, a few shrubs and flower-dotted bushes were standing here and there.

But that wasn't what held Ihon's attention.

On the opposite end of the coutyard stood the Keep, its enormous size reaching around two hundred feet the stranger guessed. Inlaid in the middle of its base were the largest doors Ihon had ever seen.

Their ebony wooden bodies, attached to their frames by black iron arms, stood like guardians against all outsiders.

Standing on either side were two statues of Wolf-Born soldiers. Their spears standing in front, gripped by their giant hands.

Ranvir slid off his saddle, boot-shod feet barely making a sound on the marble pavement.

Ihon followed likewise, though he was certain everyone in the city probably heard his landing.

Tying their horses to a hitching post standing next to the front gate, the two travellers headed across the courtyard. Once they arrived at the front doors, the two stood there in silence for a brief moment while Ihon took in the sight.

When both statues moved, Ihon couldn't help but gasp.

He had to snort to keep from laughing at himself while he watched the sentries step in front of them, turning their backs to the visitors.

The mammoth doors groaned until they gaped open, inviting the two inside.

Ranvir turned to Ihon, a smile spreading his lips.

"Welcome to the Capital."

12

Entering the dim interior, Ihon tried to catch himself before he gasped again. He had never seen such an ornately-decorated room in all his days.

The main room appeared to take up the entire base level of the Keep, stretching out in a circular pattern with a diameter of, at least, seventy feet.

It dawned on Ihon the walls were not exactly cut in a circular shape, rather an octagonal. In each corner stood a large lamp, flickering flames lighting the windowless room.

Covering the floor were around a dozen Persian rugs along with half that many bear skins, complete with snarling heads.

There were a few maplewood tables with well-crafted chairs.

Along the wall several deer and boar heads were mounted, giving the room a Royal taste. Here and there, swords or battle axes were held in antler frames.

Dotting small cherrywood platforms were various artifacts from all over the known world.

Ihon turned to speak to Ranvir, finding no words, he raised his hands in the air and chuckled.

Ranvir was still grinning. Motioning his friend to follow him, he marched across the width of the room. Stepping up to a blank stone slab set into the wall, he began reciting something, his voice chanting into the stillness.

Ihon remained as still as a statue, not daring to breathe. Listening to the words of the recitation, he recognised the similarities between Latin, Scots Gaelic, and Greek.

Must be that Wolf-Born language he wrote in that invitation to me, Ihon mused. His eyes then widened when he watched the stone slab start to turn.

Spinning slowly on its base, the carved chunk of smooth rock scraped by. Until it had opened parallel doorways, the stone did not stop.

Ranvir walked through the one on the right, waving Ihon onward.

Clenching his jaw, Ihon stepped up onto the base. He paused for a second before walking through. Looking around, he had to keep his mouth from dropping open.

They were standing in a hallway made entirely of marble stone. Every few feet along its walls, grooves had been carved in to hold gold-handled torches.

"These are the real chambers for our Supreme Council," Ranvir explained, motioning for Ihon to follow him again as he started to his right down the hall. "That outside room is built for any visitors who happen to stumble into our secluded city."

"So this is where the governing comes from?" Ihon spoke up.

"Aye," his tour guide smiled.

A minute later, the hall opened up into an extensive cavern.

Ihon wondered if they were reaching the centre of the mountain.

Several buildings had been laid all over the cavern.

"It's like an underground fortress," Ihon remarked.

"I guess you could call it that," Ranvir raised his eyebrows. "We'll probably meet a few of the Supreme Council members once inside." With that, he ushered his friend through a set of doors.

Entering a small passageway, the two were approached by four men, each wearing cloaks similar to Ranvir's but in various colours.

"Greetings, Sir Iraes," each man extended his hand to the newcomer.

A lifted eyebrow from Ihon told everyone it had been awhile since anyone had referred to him by that knightly title.

"Relax, my friend," the first man smiled, shaking the befuddled stranger's hand. "We have known of you for awhile, never sure where you were though. I am Noran Mars, a younger cousin of your grandfather, Justineus. I met your father, Justin, once during the Second Great War."

Ihon studied the man's grisled face.

"Noran recently became Chief Councilman," Ranvir spoke up at Ihon's side.

"And this," Noran turned to an elderly man. "Is our eldest member of the Supreme Council, Bhaltair Duncan. He's a thousand and fifty years old as of yesterday."

"Bloody Scottish wolf," the elder man, spat at Noran. His glare transformed into a warm smile when he shook Ihon's hand. "You're as young as you feel. I feel fifty."

A round of guffaws erupted around the group.

Ihon smiled.

"I am honoured to meet you, Sir," he replied.

"The honour is mine, to meet the son of such a hero as Justin Iraes," the old man brushed his white pony tail over his shoulder when he glanced at Ranvir. "Now we have both hero's sons, Justin and Brian."

"You're a hero yourself, Bhaltair," Ranvir patted the man on the shoulder.

"Ach," Bhaltair shrugged off the compliment. "I've lived long enough to have known the students of Christ's Apostles. I fought through the wars all over Europe, even our own Second Great War — the problem with being Wolf-Born, you don't get to keep the scars, because your wounds heal too fast."

A chuckle rippled through the group at this statement.

It was then a younger man with a thick red beard stepped forward and shook Ihon's hand with vigour.

"Angus McKlean," he introduced himself. He was a

true specimen of the Gaelicised Wolf-Born. Standing maybe an inch shorter than Ihon, he was everything that makes a warrior, bulging muscles to prove it.

"He's the baby of our Council," it was Bhaltair's turn to tease. He grabbed Angus by the shoulders and playfully shook him.

Ihon grinned, he loved how these strangers felt like family already. Turning to the last of the four, a silent figure, dressed in darker hues, he reached out his hand.

"And you are?"

Though there were smile lines around his eyes, the man remaind stoic. He accepted the offered hand and gripped it.

"Malcolm Norris."

It was then the meeting was interrupted by four more individuals, one of which was a woman who looked to be in her early thirties—Ihon was uncertain. Now that he knew his kind did not age like humans, he wondered if there might be a century or two added to that number.

"Sir Iraes," Angus stepped up to the woman who carried a braided head of hair sharing the same colour as his beard. "This is my sister, Merryn."

"I am honoured to meet you, me lady," Ihon bowed at the waist.

"The two of them are the Chroniclers for the Supreme Council," Noran spoke up, informing the new arrival. "They keep track of everything."

"And do a smashing job of it, if you ask me," Bhaltair winked at the two young siblings.

The other three Councilmen were introduced before anything else took place.

So many names, Ihon's brain screamed. I'm never going to remember them all. Unless I live here for the rest of my thousand years of life or more. I'm already in love with this place, but I'm not sure I want to do that. I miss home. I miss you, Joanna. I miss our children. How come we couldn't have all lived here? Happy and safe. It would have been a wonderful life.

His eyes turned to Ranvir.

His friend must have read the plea in them because he cleared his throat.

"Well," Ranvir rested his right hand on Ihon's shoulder. "I do believe I should take our visitor on a tour of the place."

"Very well," Angus shrugged. He bid Ihon farewell.

The rest did the same.

In minutes, they were alone, meandering down the hall.

"Are Merryn and Angus over a hundred?" Ihon broke the silence.

Ranvir laughed out loud, shaking his head.

"No," he finally managed to reply. "Merryn turned fifty-one this past spring."

Ihon raised an eyebrow. Figuring out someone's age, someone who was a Wolf-Born, was going to be a trial and a half for him until the end of time. He just knew this.

"Angus is three years younger than she."

Nodding, Ihon followed with another question, "So age has nothing to do with whether someone is elected to the

Supreme Council or not? I assume they're elected? Or is it passed on by blood as the kings of the humans do it?"

"Nay, they are elected. We did away with succession a long time ago. I do believe it was even the second Supreme Council that passed the tradition of electing our leaders based on merit instead of family ties."

"Something humans would probably find most beneficial," Ihon remarked.

"This is true," Ranvir agreed. He glanced over his shoulder, raising his eyebrows.

Ihon heard the two as they approached in a scuffle.

"What are you doing?" Ranvir questioned the siblings.

Angus chuckled, "Merryn and I decided we wanted to help with the tour, figured it would be a good idea to get to know this new friend of ours."

Adjusting the sheathed sword that was belted to her slender waist over the green satin gown she was wearing, Merryn held Ihon's face in her gaze. Her lips curled in a soft smile.

Ranvir glanced from Angus to Merryn then to Ihon. He shrugged.

Ihon shrugged.

"What is this?" Angus cocked an eyebrow. "Some kind of shrugging party? Come on, let's go!" With that he scurried off down a connecting hallway, the group following on his haunches.

"They act like children," Ranvir retorted under his breath to Ihon.

"Excuse me, Sir," Merryn narrowed her green eyes at Ranvir. "He acts like a child, I, however, am keeping to the principles of a high-class lady."

"Yes," Ihon found himself smiling at the pseudo-haughty look plastered on her face. "That you are, me lady."

"Call me Merryn, Sir Iraes."

"So long as you call me by my given name, Merryn."

"As you wish, Sir Ihon,"

"My title does not matter, it has been years since the last Crusade."

"What is all this banter I hear," Angus froze in his footsteps and turned to face the trio. "I thought we were giving Ihon a tour?"

"Right you are," Ranvir chuckled. He winked at Ihon before scurrying up to Angus's side and rounding a corner in the hall.

Merryn turned the corner behind the two, her braid managing to brush against Ihon's arm as he followed.

It was at this juncture that the hallway broke off into three different paths.

"We have three wings in this fortress," Angus spoke up.

"As obvious as that is," Ranvir nudged his younger friend. Then glancing over his shoulder at Ihon, he continued. "We'll start with the Judgment Hall." Facing left, he motioned their tourist to follow.

"Judgment Hall?" Ihon repeated the name, arching an eyebrow. "That sounds foreboding."

Merryn gigled at his side.

"It could be, if you are one of those who don't behave."

Ihon glanced sideways at the redhaired beauty. Was she flirting with him?

"The Judgment Hall is where the Supreme Council convenes for trials, deliberations, and other higher meetings," Ranvir informed. "It is also where we enlist newcomers."

"Enlist?" Ihon turned to his friend.

"Basically," Angus cut in. "Even though you're a Wolf-Born, in order for the People of the Creed to accept you, there are some recitations and swearing in that have to be met first."

"Recitations? Swearing in?" Ihon was raising both eyebrows when he stepped up to the open doorway and peered inside.

The room was constructed to look like a Greek amphitheatre. Its capacity could seat around two thousand people, Ihon surmised. Down at the front and centre were eight throne-like seats carved from marble, glistening like pearls.

"Remember the Ancient Creed I was telling you about?" Ranvir reminded. "You will have to memorise it and recite it in a hearing before the Supreme Council. Then, if you decide to, you will swear allegiance to it and volunteer your loyalty to the Wolf-Born Race."

"Sounds emphatic," Ihon muttered, pulling back. He glanced from one face to the next of his tour guides.

Angus shrugged.

Ranvir smiled, "I believe it will be nothing to you. I've already guessed you to be a man of upright character, possessing the greatest of virtues."

"Trying to flatter me, Ranvir?" Ihon smirked.

It was Merryn's turn to join in.

"I don't think so, Ranvir has always been a good judge of character and I too see you as a good man."

Ihon could only nod, unsure of how to respond to the compliments.

"Follow me," Angus broke into the silence. He hurried back up the hallway. "The west wing takes us to the Hall of Heroes."

"Now that sounds inspiring," a smile spread over Ihon's mouth.

Ranvir chuckled.

The next door was opened and the four stepped through.

The Hall of Heroes turned out to be a gargantuan room with a museum-like air, statues and plaques lining up and standing in all corners of the spacious cavern.

Ranvir stepped up to a white marble monument of two armoured warriors walking together with their arms on each other's shoulders.

"Can you guess who these two men are?" He pointed at the creations, smiling at Ihon.

Unable to find his voice, Ihon stared at the statues. Everything was taking his breath away, the splendour of all the precious craftsmanship was near too much for him. He then saw a familiar Scottish claymore carved onto the back of the warrior on the right.

When the look of recognition blanketed his face, Ranvir's grin cut wider. He nodded.

"This monument was christened forty years ago in memorium for our two fathers, brothers-in-arms, they fought and died for the preservation of our Race as you know. Heroes to the end, they live on in this Hall as well as in our veins, my friend."

Ihon managed to breathe deeply. He also discovered his feet could finally move and started meandering down the aisles of statues and monuments. Coming upon a single figure who carried what appeared to be a sceptre, a round stone at his feet, Ihon paused.

Fingers brushed his arm.

Turning to gaze down at Merryn, Ihon listened as she explained this memorial.

"That is Kalran the Originator, he is the first-born of our Race. Tiras and Kissa, the progenitors of our People, birthed four sons and four daughters. With Kalran as their chief, they founded the first Supreme Council — the ones to write down the Ancient Creed and build the first Sanguiatro."

"Amazing," Ihon mumbled. He studied the statue, a tingle climbing his arms and reaching the back of his neck. Standing among the ghosts of heroes, he felt so unworthy.

"You'll be able to spend more time in here over the next three days," Angus's voiced hewed into the moment of reverie. He started for the door.

"Three days?" Ihon questioned, turning to the exiting Councilman.

"Yes," Merryn nodded, ushering their guest forward. "That's the required number of days to allow newcomers to study the past and make their decision about pledging to the Creed."

"Oh," Ihon nodded. "Sounds more doable than what I was expecting."

"It pays to be Wolf-Born too," Ranvir spoke up as they left the room, their footsteps echoing across the outside walls while they followed Angus to the next wing. "We don't need as much sleep as humans do, giving us more time to research and learn."

"Amazing," Ihon muttered. "I'd always wondered about that. Never seemed to have an issue with not getting enough sleep—during the war, there were times I went nights without it and only needed a few hours to recharge afterward. Probably why I was promoted quickly, my fellow knights called me the king of vigilence."

With that he chuckled, the memories flooding his already overloaded brain.

"This last door," Angus grabbed the handle. "Leads us to, one of Merryn's favourites in all the city, the Hall of Origins."

The door opened to reveal a room filled to the brim of bookshelves and desks covered in scrolls and leather-bound tomes. The amount of knowledge was almost tangible inside.

Stepping through, Ihon found his lungs struggling to take in oxygen, the sheer awestruck wonder sent his pulse into an erratic race.

"You'll be able to spend as much time in here as you wish over the next three days," Ranvir informed. "Learning the histories of our Race will do you good. It'll give you the aide you need to make a firm decision for your future."

Ihon opened his mouth, finding no words.

"I remember the same feeling," Merryn's voice was near a whisper. "When I first came here. Your excitement is making me thrilled all over again. I can literally feel it emanating from you."

Ihon was too transfixed on the books to respond to her remark.

"Well," Angus grinned. "I guess, we'll leave you to it. The room you'll be staying is back down the hall toward the front where it connects with the outside Keep. If you get lost, just ask the next person you see, there are a few other guests from the city who like to roam the halls in meditation or study."

When they received a nod of confirmation from Ihon, the three departed without a sound, leaving him to his own devices.

The next three days were going to be an overload of information.

Stepping up to a pedastal carrying a large volume bound in leather, Ihon reached up and opened the cover. His eyes scanned the page the tome happened to open to. Goose bumps jumping up his spine, he caught his breath at the words he read.

13

Cato Iraes was the last of Ihon's lineage to have a seat on the Supreme Council. His son, Justineus remained behind in Rome during the first phase of the Second Migration—the time when Sanguiatro moved to its present location in the Scottish Highlands. Justineus was a Roman centurion who was sent to Jerusalem.

Ihon reread the last sentence in the tome. He then read it a third time, unable to believe his eyes.

Justineus was the Roman centurion, in the gospel of Matthew, who went to Christ and asked for the healing of his servant. Christ had been amazed at the faith of this Roman.

Ihon's eyes lifted from the page and stared off at nothing in the room.

"My grandfather was mentioned in the Holy Scriptures," he muttered under his breath. The pulsing ripples zipping up his arm sent a trickle of sweat down his forehead. To be related to someone who actually spoke with God during his days walking this earth, what an honour.

"Almighty," Ihon looked to the ceiling. "I am so unworthy. Who am I to be the heir of such a line?"

A page rustled in an open book nearby.

Funny, Ihon mused. A breeze inside a closed room.

He then turned back to his reading.

The hours ticked by while the visitor moved from one work to another. There were so many artifacts of knowledge. One scroll mentioned the existence of what were called the "Eight Letters of Tiras."

Apparently, the Father of the Wolf-Born Race had written each letter to each of his eight children.

Next came the Chronicles of the Supreme Council. Each scroll possessed the record of each generation of the council, outlining the events during each era.

Ihon's stomach growled.

Rolling the scroll up, he rubbed the bridge of his nose.

Time for supper, he thought. I wonder if there is a banquet hall or would they have food ready in my quarters?

With that, his feet took him down the hallway toward the front.

His nose told him there was definitely food waiting for him. In less than a minute, he'd found his room.

The lavish decorations of tiger and fox fur rugs, the blue tapestries draped across the black brick walls, the gothic theme to the room's designs did not register in the mind of the new ravenous tenant.

Lying out on a birchwood table next to the oak bed, was a silver platter holding the roasted carcase of a large boar.

Ihon's mouth watered, drool teasing the corners of his lips. He plopped down on the floor, next to the low-set table and tore into the meal. Letting his fangs extend, he savoured the fresh warm meat with every devouring bite.

Over the course of the next three days, Ihon found himself moving from the Hall of Heroes to the Hall of Origins countless times. He would usually take a scroll or book with him and hang with the statues of the legends.

Sometime near the middle of the afternoon on the third day, he told himself he needed a break.

A bit of fresh air would do you some good, he remarked to himself.

In minutes, he was outside the Keep, trudging across the courtyard, through the front gates, and down into the city. His steps took him through the marketplace. After buying a fresh-roasted rabbit with the few coins he'd managed to bring with him on his trip, he ate his supper and continued on down the streets. Tossing the emptied stick aside after smacking his lips from the last bite, he glanced around.

Surrounding him were several stone houses, apparently he'd walked into the residential part of town.

"You look a bit lost, stranger," a shaky voice cut into his thoughts.

Ihon turned, his dark eyes alighting on an elderly woman sitting outside the front door of her house. This one was half wood, half stone — quite ornate in its design. He smiled and gave a bow to her.

"I've been couped up inside the Keep, preparing for my ceremony of allegiance — I guess that's what you would call it. I needed a break and took a walk."

"Well, come sit with me," the woman smiled, her eyes wrinkling. "What's your name?"

"Ihon Iraes," he smiled, stepping up to her porch. Taking the chair that was offered to him, he asked, "What is yours?"

"I'm Sarah," she continued grinning, eyes twinkling. Brushing a strand of silver hair out of her face, she studied Ihon.

"Are you Wolf-Born?" He asked, his eyes taking in her worn features.

She chuckled, knowing his reasoning behind the question.

"Aye," she nodded. "I am. I may not look as young and spry as most of our people, that's because, though we age slower than humans, we still age nonetheless."

"So that means," Ihon's voice trailed off. A bit of heat rose in his cheeks.

"That I'm old?" Sarah snickered. She winked at Ihon. "No need to concern yourself over offending me. I am old. Everyone gets old — humans and Wolf-Born. Though, God shortened mankind's lifespan to average seventy years, extending ours to eleven hundred. I've reached one thousand and eighty-nine — it's been a good long life and I'm happy for it."

"You're older than..." Ihon racked his brain, but he couldn't remember the name.

"Bhaltair?" Sarah finished for him. "The oldest of the Supreme Council? Yes, yes I am. To me, he was still a young pup when he was elected to that post."

"Did you know my father or grandfather perhaps?" Ihon had to ask. "Justin Iraes, his father's name was Justineus, he was a Roman centurion."

"I knew of both of them, never got the pleasure or honour of meeting them though. I'm sorry."

"No need to be sorry," Ihon shrugged. "I was just wondering."

"I did, however, meet Cato — your great-grandfather."

Ihon's eyes must have widened to an unnatural diameter because Sarah broke into a fit of laughter.

She swatted her knee as she rocked back in her chair. When she finally calmed herself, she remarked.

"You look a bit like him. Same eyes, the Roman nose is a given, and if I imagined you without a beard, the resemblance might be uncanny."

"He didn't have a beard?" Ihon raised an eyebrow, such a seemingly insignifcant feature he found interesting.

"No," Sarah shook her head, pursing her lips. "Beards were not a thing among the higher class at that time. Rome was founded around the time of old Cato's birth actually. I guess, they found beards too burdensome while building such a great city."

Here her eyes moved to the distance, recalling some thousand-year-old memory.

"Did you know him well?" Ihon felt a bit rude for interrupting the reminiscing, he couldn't help it.

"I guess you could call us close aquaintences," Sarah shrugged. "I was busy at the time raising a family of three sons and two daughters. He was more friends with my brother's family at the time, focused on keeping the secret of our Race from the curious minds of the founders of Rome at the time. We were trying to help build a city without being noticed, you know."

"Intriguing," Ihon nodded, leaning back in his chair. "I'm told we also built Constantinople?"

"Yes," Sarah grinned. "And Troy, though I wasn't around at that time. By the time I came along, that great city had been destroyed—mostly by its own wickedness."

Silence then took over for a moment as the elder recollected the glory days and the young processed the given information.

"Anyways," Sarah took a deep breath. "You tell me tonight is your hearing? Do you know what your decision is going to be?"

Ihon smiled. He did know, he'd known before his studies ever began. It just took his mind three days to realise what his heart was telling him. With a nod, he answered.

"Yes. I do believe I've already made it."

"Excellent," the elderly woman clapped her hands. "Then I'll be sure to be there. Now, the hearing will take place tonight. It will only last for a few minutes, they'll take you to a back room where the Stone of the Ancient Creed lies. You'll be given the entire night to memorise the Laws written on that Stone. Then, the actual ceremony takes place at sunrise tomorrow morning. I'll see you then, my friend."

"Wave to me," Ihon stood to his feet, bowed, then marched back up the street, making his way back up the mountainside to the waiting arms of the Keep. His mind raced as he thought of what was about to happen. This was a decision that would change the rest of his life — however long that would be.

14

Opening with a gavel bang, Noran, the Chief Councilman, stared down at the man before him on the platform. Noran, along with the rest of the Supreme Council were seated in their marble thrones, peering down at Ihon who stood in front of the circular stone seats in the Judgment Hall.

"You've made your decision then?" Noran's gaze was grim.

Ihon met the stare with a set jaw. He nodded.

"I have."

"Very well," came the swift response. "You will be given this night to memorise the codes of the Ancient Creed. At sunrise, on the morrow, you will stand before your peers and this Council to give your oath of allegiance to the Creed and your loyalty to the Wolf-Born Race. Is this understood?"

"It is."

Noran motioned for Bhaltair, who was seated next to the Chief Councilman, to usher Ihon off the platform.

The older Wolf-Born descended the stone steps at the base of his throne. He took Ihon by the arm and escorted him to a metallic door that was nearly hidden by the Council seats. Opening the large door, Bhaltair motioned for Ihon to enter the dimly-lit interior.

Once Ihon was inside, the door shut behind him and he was left alone.

The room was in a triangular shape, one torch burning in each of the three corners, giving the occupant enough light to see that large smooth stone sitting on a small platform in the middle of the room.

The words etched across its face were, naturally, in the Wolf-Born tongue. This Creed was for their Race and theirs alone.

Ihon stepped closer to the rock.

I wonder if the reason it seems similar to the Gaelic, Latin, and Greek languages, is because our People helped with those foundations.

His mind mulled this thought over.

It would make sense then that this language is their originator. What a fascinating idea. I'll have to ask someone later.

Kneeling down in front of the platform, Ihon ran his finger across the carved letters. He mouthed the words, feeling like he shouldn't actually speak them out loud. The stirring they sent into his very core, gave them a sacred and hallowed air.

The nightly hours passed quickly. By the time the sun peeked over the horizon outside of the mountain, Ihon could recite the laws beginning to end and backward without one glimpse at the age-old stone.

The door opened with a loud groan.

"Are you ready, Sir Ihon?" Bhaltair's voice echoed from outside.

"I am," Ihon stepped into the brighter light of the amphitheatre. Blinking quickly, his vision adjusting to the interior, he approached the stage in front of the Council's ring of stones. Catching his breath, he stared at the crowd that was now gathering on the seats surrounding the platform.

Hundreds were attending this ceremony.

A hand waved from over on the left side, about halfway up the stands. It was Sarah, her wizened face beaming down at him.

Ihon returned the smile before turning to face the Supreme Council, his back to the audience.

Once Bhaltair finished ascending to his seat, Noran thundered.

"Ihon Iraes, son of the Wolf-Born Race, what say you?"

For a moment, Ihon was certain every single person in the room was holding their breath. When he cleared his throat, it sounded like a lightning bolt.

"I, Ihon Iraes, do solemnly swear my allegiance to the Ancient Creed and its laws. I give my utmost loyalty to the Wolf-Bon Race, the People of the Creed. I will uphold the laws, upon finishing the recitation of the Creed, I bind my body, soul, and mind to it, so help me, God."

With that, there was a slight trickle of shifting in the

seats behind him. Everyone was anticipating the recitation. This was a holy event, unheard of by any human ears and never allowed outside of these chambers.

Ihon began, the words felt natural to his tongue, rolling off and out of his mouth as he spoke them. He could see each line in his mind's eyes as if the stone were still in front of him.

Every observer, including each of the eight members of the Supreme Council, hung on to his every word.

Minutes later, Ihon finished. He took a breath and waited.

Noran studied the newcomer. His grim features slowly changed.

A twinkle started in his deep gray eyes, spreading out into a grin that cut his narrow mouth.

"Welcome, Brother," he muttered. Grabbing the gavel once more, he slammed it down in a firm, swift clang that reverberated across the seats and walls of the Hall.

Ihon found himself grinning.

Merryn and Angus nearly jumped from their thrones, descending the few stone stairs between themselves and their new friend. They congratulated him with hugs and laughter.

Ranvir joined in, he'd been seated on the front row of the audience. His grin looked like it could reach his ears and slice his face in half. He swatted Ihon on the back.

"Well done, my friend," he chuckled. "Well done. I knew you'd make it."

"Did you ever doubt me?" Ihon tilted his head.

"Never," Ranvir smirked.

"I'm proud of you, son," Sarah's voice joined in the raucous. "Your ancestors are proud too, I'm certain."

The group turned to the elder lady, all the men gave her respectful bows.

"Thank you," Ihon nodded his head, his eyes to the floor.

"Rise up, I'm just an old woman," she winked at Merryn while the men stood upright. "Now, everyone is invited to my home for a celebratory feast in our new friend's honour."

"Oh no," Ihon raised both hands. "You don't have to do that."

"We want to, Brother," Ranvir patted his friend on the arm. "It's not every day one of our own is enlisted into our fold by way of ceremony. It's actually very rare for a Wolf-Born to be unaware of who and what he is as long as you have."

"As you wish then," Ihon muttered after a moment of thought. "Thank you."

With that, the party exited the Hall, making sure to invite the rest of the Supreme Council to the feast. The next few hours passed, bringing on the afternoon then the evening at which time the party was to start.

A few toasts were given around the longest table Ihon had ever laid eyes on, it bore more dishes and platters of food than he could ever count in one sitting.

Near the end of the meal, Noran and Bhaltair approached Ihon who was chatting with his group of new friends amidst sharing a large vat of fowl stew.

"Sir Ihon," Noran interrupted. "The Supreme Council would like to extend an offer to you."

Ranvir was sitting opposite Ihon at the table — he looked up at the two and raised his left eyebrow.

Ihon had to turn around to face the Councilmen.

"Yes?" He asked.

Bhaltair broke into his grandfatherly grin, he winked at Sarah who coyly dropped her gaze to her plate before her.

Noran continued, "At present, there are twenty-four Lesser Officers of the Creed Order. I'm sure you've been informed that your father was actually a Higher Officer back during the last Great War. There are only nine of that rank now. We would like to offer you the rank of Lesser Officer. Ranvir can give you the details and responsibilities required for the office. We have quite a few assignments coming up and need another set of hands."

Ihon glanced over his shoulder at Ranvir who smiled in return. His mind racing, Ihon turned back to the two waiting men.

Everything was feeling like a whirlwind, flying by so fast.

He felt as if he barely had enough time to grab a hold of each new revelation. Would he even be able to meet their standards with this position? How soon would he have to begin his duties?

"I think you can do it, Ihon," Merryn whispered at his side.

Ihon met her look. He clenched his jaw. Turning to the Councilmen, he cleared his throat. Yet another decision to make that would alter his life. Could he do it?

15

oments like these made the world feel as if it had increased its spin, he was certain his entire body would fracture then burst into a billion pieces. Ihon met the gazes of the two men still waiting for his decision.

"I'll do it," he shocked himself with the firmness of his own voice.

"Excellent," Bhaltair smiled down, reaching for his hand, the old man shook it. "I knew you would. Congratulations, son."

Noran nodded, his emotions were a bit less obvious. He gave Ihon a nod of approval before turning to Ranvir.

"You will explain the duties to our new Lesser Officer of the Creed Order then?"

"Aye, Sir," Ranvir bobbed his head up and down. As the two headed off back up to the Keep, he grinned at his friend. "Now we share the same rank. Look at you though, it took me three years before I was offered this position. You've been here, what? Four days? And here you are already at my level."

"No need to get jealous, Ranvir," Angus chuckled. "The ranks only matter during times of war anyway. We're all equal besides that."

"I'm not jealous," Ranvir winked at the younger. "Just envious, before you know it, they'll be promoting our new friend to Higher Officer, like his father. He may even become a Supreme Council member for all we know."

Ihon shook his head. He could feel his face burning red, the heat smoldering under his cheeks.

Everything had taken such a different turn. His life was so different.

~

The days following Ihon's acceptance into city life of Sanguiatro turned into weeks. Ihon settled in across the street from Sarah's house. He and Cassieus got along well with the peaceful life around them.

Day to day business was almost a ritual. Ihon would either spend it studying in the Hall of Origins, or hang out with new friends he made along the way in the city. At the beginning of the week, he found, was the best time to visit the market. Though most people would drop by the stalls every other day — he was told there was no point stocking up for the week, seeing as they always had abundance.

Those weeks turned into years.

It felt as if God snapped His fingers.

One afternoon, a couple weeks after his eightieth birthday, Ihon was sitting in a whicker chair on his front porch, dozing off.

"Officer Iraes," a voiced boomed into his lazy dream.

Nearly diving to the porch floor, Ihon bolted upright. His eyes a bit foggy, he blinked twice until he could make out the features of the man standing a few yards in front of him in the street.

"Angus," he recognised his friend. "It's been awhile. What brings you back to Sanguiatro?"

"I've been on a mission beyond the Carpathian mountains in Eastern Europe, just finished." Angus smiled, but something was eating him on the inside, it was obvious.

"What's the matter, my friend?" Ihon dropped his grin.

"The Supreme Council finally has a task for you," Angus informed. He cleared his throat.

"Sounds good to my ears, I've been getting lazy these days," Ihon stood up, stepping over to the edge of the porch.

"You remember those eight Elite Rogues we told you about?"

"Yes," Ihon nodded, he felt a pang slicing into his heart. "I executed one of them, according to Ranvir, after he took my wife."

"Aye," Angus dropped his gaze to the ground. He never liked bringing up a painful topic, who would? Returning to meet his friend's curious look, he continued. "We've received word that a second one has been discovered."

Jumping from the porch to the ground, Ihon approached the Council Chronicler.

"Where?"

"He's overtaken the Holy Land recently."

Ihon raised both eyebrows, gaping at Angus.

"Aye," the Councilman clenched his teeth, nodding. It was like he was reading his friend's thoughts. "The very one, Saladin."

Without a moment's hesitation, Ihon asked, "How soon can I leave?"

Angus took a breath, he seemed taken aback at the speed of his friend's decision. He then shrugged, a bit hesitant.

"We'll convene in an hour to brief you on your mission. I'll see you then," with that, he hurried back up the road in the direction of the Keep.

"Right," Ihon nodded. He then turned and headed inside his house. Gathering a few belongings, he belted on a gray tunic he'd bought at the market on his last visit.

The fabric was comfortable and blended with the newly-crafted black leather belt and sheath for his claymore.

Strapping on the sheath, Ihon grinned as he ran his finger down the long blade of the old sword.

Finally, he thought. I can get into some action. It's been a long time coming.

By the time the hour had ended, Ihon was standing outside of the Judgment Hall, waiting. He ran his left hand through the long mane of hair he kept tied behind his shoulders in a black string. Why did it always seem to take forever for things to happen no matter what government you were working with? He wondered.

It was then, the door opened.

Angus stood on the other side, ushering him in. He followed right behind the officer while he approached the platform.

"Ihon," Noran spoke from his seat. "You've already accepted to take the mission to assassinate the next Elite Rogue, Saladin?"

"Aye," Ihon realised he might be nodding his head with a bit too much vigour and stopped.

"Now we know you've already received training for the needed skills," the Chief Councilman continued. "Will you be using your sword to do the job?"

"I was considering using the poison—the only one able to slay a Wolf-Born, hemlace juice?"

"Such a dark plan," Noran shifted in his seat. "Why do you wish to go that route?"

"There is word that King Richard the First of England is leading a third Crusade to the Holy Land in an attempt to reclaim it?"

"Aye, this is true."

"I've considered it best to accompany his forces. But, once there, it will be difficult to get near Saladin."

Bhaltair spoke up, his eyebrows furrowed, "You think the only way is to allow yourself to be captured possibly? Maybe you'll gain audience with the Elite Rogue?"

"This is my idea," Ihon replied, his mouth flat.

"Risky," the older Wolf-Born stroked his long white beard. He glanced to his side at Noran.

Noran shrugged.

"It might work," Bhaltair muttered. Though he kept his tone low, the echo from the amphitheatre still amplified it.

"Sounds like a plan to me," Noran shrugged again. "You have the permission, the charge, and the authority of the Supreme Council backing you. Go, and by God's Grace, we'll see you when you return."

Giving a bow, Ihon backed up the stands and exited the room. His mouth set, he steeled his own resolve. Making his way back to his house, he quickly saddled the young black stallion waiting in his stables.

As he mounted and the steed stepped out of the enclosed stall, Ihon's eyes fell on the square tombstone set up next to a tree just a few feet to the side of the stable.

"Cassieus, my old friend," he muttered, his mind going back in time. "It seems I'm heading off on a new Crusade. I wish you could go with me. I know you'd be excited to get back into battle. I miss you, my friend."

The young horse beneath dipped his head as if in salute to the grave.

"Seneca," Ihon peered down at the three-year old. "It appears you and I have a great partnership ahead of us. Are you ready to carry me into battle, young one?"

The stallion whinnied as he bobbed his long neck up and down.

Snickering, Ihon shook his head. With that, he nudged the mount forward into a charge down the road. But the grin dissipated within minutes when the sobering thought of the task ahead gripped the rider's chest. Could he go up against a second Elite? Could he pull this off without giving away his identity and that of his Race to the countless humans he'd be traveling and fighting with? Only time would tell.

16

Evening moved over the land as the lone rider trailed across the rolling hills of northern England. Perhaps by the next time the sun set, he would make London.

Maybe I should have left my horse and traveled on foot, Ihon thought to himself. It would definitely have taken less time. But perhaps, when I arrive, King Richard will be ready to leave?

Seneca was tired. His long black mane a bit matted from the sweat of the day's trip.

"Okay, my young friend," Ihon patted his ride. "We'll stop here on this hill tonight. But we leave at sunrise, so you better get your sleep." With that he dismounted and unsaddled the equine.

Seneca snorted in thanks. He trudged off, his nose in the green grass, grazing. Within minutes after his supper, he was asleep.

Ihon sat cross-legged, overlooking the landscape.

This part of the island was blanketed in forests, even

the lakes looked small compared to the immense armies of trees all around.

Barely able to see more than a mile from his perch, the Wolf-Born used his sense of smell. He could tell what was around him in that ten-mile radius.

There was a flock of sheep about five miles to the east of his position. They were most likely tucked in for the night in what smelled like an old barn next to a thatched hut. The roof on the hut had been given a fresh batch of straw.

He smiled at the scent of the wet forest just a few yards away.

The underbrush was doused in dew and the mist from that morning's rain.

A twig snapped somewhere half a mile inside the forest, causing the listener's ears to perk up.

Though not in his Beast form, Ihon still found himself reacting like a wolf. His ears felt so tiny in his human form, he despised not being able to move them to hear better as he could in the other form.

The clouds above parted, revealing a dozen pinpoints of light plastered on the black canvas.

Ihon leaned back until he was stretched out on the ground, slipping his hands up behind his head, he smiled up at the sky. He'd always loved the stars.

The hours ticked by.

Finally, a rooster crowed back at the barn so many miles away.

Ihon sat up, he didn't remember dozing off.

A pink hue was streaked across the horizon just above the treeline. It looked like the Almighty's giant finger had dipped into paint and traced the outline of the hills.

Plunging his hand inside his saddle bags, Ihon searched for the last roasted rabbit he'd packed for the trip.

I need to do some more hunting before I join the Lionhearted's army, he told himself as he gulped down the tender meat. Once finished, he jumped to his feet, tossed the carcase to the ground, and picked up his saddle.

Seneca gave a shake of his head in waking. He stretched his long legs when seeing his master approaching.

"It's time to awaken, my friend. We have another long day's ride ahead of us. I want to make London by this evening."

The young horse whinnied.

"I know, I'm kind of weary of traveling myself," Ihon strapped the saddle onto his mount's back. "But, we might as well get used to it, seeing as we still have a longer trip even after London. We're going all the way to the Holy Land."

Seneca did not seem impressed but he made no more protestations.

Swinging up into the leather seat, Ihon pulled on the reins and nudged his heels into the horse's ribs.

Within minutes, they were trotting across the countryside. After half an hour, they passed that thatched hut.

Ihon stared at the flock of sheep.

Bleating inside the corral, the dull faces gazed at him.

They appeared to be a bit put out at him for having awakened them so early.

Ihon grinned, catching himself before he licked his lips.

Oh, how a fresh lamb stew would taste so good, he mused.

His stomach growled.

Urging his steed on a bit faster, Ihon focused on the trail ahead.

The sun climbed into the sky, its warmth showering the English forests. An afternoon salt breeze from the sea swept over while the star descended.

Before Ihon knew it, the evening was coming on. He could barely make out the city structures etched against the horizon.

"We're almost there, Seneca," Ihon broke into a grin. The idea gave him a bit more energy.

It seemed to give his stallion more energy, the young steed broke into a soft gallop.

Within minutes, the two reached the outskirts of London.

"Hail to thee, traveller," a thick-bearded man, dressed in peasant's garb and carrying a pitchfork, waved his left hand at Ihon.

"Hail, friend," Ihon gave a slight bow of his chin. "Could you tell me if King Richard has departed for the Crusade yet?"

"Nay," the man smirked. "His forces plan to leave on the morrow, or so I'm told. Be you a knight?"

"Aye," Ihon nodded. "I'm a knight."

"His Majesty will be pleased with that. I hear he's been a bit ill-tempered with all the peasants and pages joining his forces. I do believe he wishes for more knights or men-at-arms."

"It would make sense," Ihon shrugged while Seneca passed the man. He waved over his shoulder. "Godspeed, stranger."

"Godspeed, Knight." The peasant bowed and went on his way.

The smells of the city filled Ihon's nostrils with their rancid putridness.

Bile burned the back of his throat.

"I hate cities," he muttered to no one in particular.

Seneca's hooves clapped against the cobblestone streets as they made their way deeper into the human-infested grounds.

"Why is it," Ihon spoke to his horse in a low tone. "When humans pile themselves up together in cities, they always end up raising so much filth? Their disgusting scents taint God's creation."

Seneca shook his head and snorted.

Ihon chuckled.

"Sir Knight," a young female voice called out.

Turning in its direction, Ihon rested his eyes on a pretty young lass dressed in a decent gown but still wearing quite a few dirt smears on her slender frame.

"Do you seek His Majesty's forces?" She looked up at

him through long red eyelashes.

"Aye," Ihon gave her a bow from atop his mount.

"He is just down that street to your right," she brushed the waist-length braid of red hair behind her shoulder.

"Thank you, little lady," Ihon reached inside the small money pouch he carried on his waist. Tossing the lass a silver coin, he edged Seneca onward down the directed street.

The sounds of brawling and hacking laughter met his ears.

"Yes, there is no doubt about it," he remarked. "We've definitely reached the army." Memories of military life flooded his brain as he rode through a ring of guards and approached a long table.

Five knights, dressed in full body armour, sat around the table chatting and guffawing like they were in a near-drunken stupour.

"Is this where I sign up?" Ihon cut into their jokes.

The group froze, staring up at the stranger. Each pair of eyes studied him from head to foot.

"You come from the northlands?" A blonde knight sat up at the left side of the table.

"Aye, I come from Scotland," Ihon made sure to pronounce that sentence with his thickest Scottish brogue. He did not much care for the looks of disdain given him from the group of English bloods.

"Very well," the blonde brushed a strand of his shoulder length hair out of his face and grabbed a quill pen. He handed it to the stranger who was now dismounting. "You can put your horse in the temporary stables with the rest of ours thirty yards to your left. We expect each knight to feed his own horse and glean it as well. There'll be no favouring anyone."

"Sounds good to me," Ihon plastered a smile on his face as he took the pen. "I'm told we're supposed to start out tomorrow?"

"Yes," the blonde nodded, his English accent clipped. "Shortly after sunrise. His Majesty wishes for everyone to be ready then."

"And what is the route he plans to take?" Ihon finished signing his name and handed the pen back.

"You will refer to him as His Majesty while in his ranks." A brunette, his arms crossed over his barrel chest and left hand caressing his beard, glared at the Scottish knight.

Ihon peered up at the other knight, he met the man's gaze. He then gave a nod—no sense arguing, he had a mission to complete and this was the best way to go about it.

"I'll be ready at sunrise," he gave a smile to the group, grabbed the reins of his steed, and headed for the stables.

〜

King Richard the Lionhearted took his volunteer forces southward out of London. In two day's ride they made it to the English Channel. The trip across the Channel by boat took a total of five days thanks to the number of horses and the size of the army.

Ihon was growing impatient, but he had to remind himself while they were crossing the French lands, everything came to you in its own time.

"We hope to make it to Crete before winter," one squire told Ihon as he helped clean the suit of armour given to the knight. The lad was a warm-mannered Welshman who took to the Scot immediately during their first week in the forces.

"Is that what you hear?" Ihon muttered, he was trying to keep from growling. The lad was doing nothing wrong, it was just the Beast inside.

I should have gone alone and in my Wolf-Born form, his brain argued. Though I would have had to go the long way around, I could have been in the Holy Land in less time than it's going to take this bloody army.

"Yes, Sir," the squire nodded. "Good time, no?"

"Right," Ihon shrugged, he found himself chuckling.

"Something funny?" The boy was only about fourteen or fifteen, his blue eyes studied the knight, eyebrows both raised.

"Nothing really," Ihon waved his hand, brushing away the query.

The boy went back to cleaning the suit of armour.

The next few days took the English army into Italion dominion where they met up with several other forces—a German emperor by the name of Barbarossa, and the French King Philip Augustus.

The leaders squabbled but a path was decided upon for each force. It took two weeks for the armies to travel down the Italian peninsula, King Richard decided it best to stop by Rome for the Pope's blessing.

It wasn't until they were passing the island of Sicily on ships that Ihon felt like he could finally breathe. From here on out it should be nothing but sailing straight to the Holy Land.

"Have you heard where we'll be making port?" He asked his squire who was busy swabbing the deck of the ship around them.

"According to Benji, the page who takes the King his breakfast every morning, His Majesty is planning to meet up with the other Crusading forces at Acre."

"Isn't that Muslim-controled?" Ihon raised an eyebrow, his gaze staying out at the glimmering sea.

"Yes," the squire squirmed.

"So," Ihon leaned against the ship's railing. "He wants to make a surprise attack. The Sultan, Saladin, would probably expect us to land somewhere in the Kingdom of Jerusalem. Sounds reckless…" Ihon's mouth parted in a narrow smile. "I like it."

Now the question is, his mind wondered. Should I help take that stronghold? Or would it be best, I sneak off during the battle and find that Elite Rogue? I wonder if maybe he'll be close by.

This mission might turn out to be a bit harder than he expected.

He wondered if he should have asked for a few teammates to come with him. Time would only tell, he guessed.

17

When the ships docked at Crete to reload their supplies, news travelled through the army about the death of Emperor Barbarossa—he'd drowned on the way there.

But this did not stay the rest of the forces. In a few short days, the French and English armies were sailing again.

When the afternoon came that held the sight of the enemy's stronghold, Ihon was pumped.

He stood at the railing, dressed in light armour, gripping the hilt of his claymore as he held it in front of him. He twirled it around, carving a small hole into the wooden plank beneath his feet.

"That greatsword will come in handy," a booming voice cut into his reverie.

Turning to face the voice's owner, Ihon's eyebrows sprang up. He dropped to one knee.

"Your Majesty," he muttered, keeping his head low. "My sword is at your beckoning."

"Rise up, Sir Knight," King Richard smiled. He pointed at the weapon and asked, "Is that one of those Scottish Claymores?"

"Aye," Ihon lifted the blade in his hands. He handed it, hilt first, to the king.

"I've never laid eyes on one, thank you," the dark-haired royal took the sword as if it were a delicate creature. His eyes studied the double-edged blade with awe. "I've heard stories though." Handing the weapon back to its owner, he turned his gaze to the distant brown-brick walls. "The fanatics use shorter weapons called scimitars, do you think your sword could beat such?"

"I believe so," Ihon couldn't help but recall the days of his service in the Second Crusade. So many heads and appendages had been sawed from their bodies by this very blade. He wondered just how many Spawn had met their deaths when his father weilded the blade during the Second Great War.

"Good," the king interrupted his wandering mind again. "We will make landfall tonight around that knoll just five miles south of the fortress. I don't think they see us just yet. If so, we have plenty of time to lay siege before they can send word for reinforcements. What is your name, Sir Knight?"

"Ihon Iraes, your Majesty."

"Sir Ihon Iraes, I look forward to fighting along side you in this upcoming battle. Godspeed." With that the king meandered off down the edge of the ship.

"Same to you," Ihon called after. Now what? He wondered. Hopefully he doesn't literally mean, side by side. Maybe I can get him to send me on a scouting party to make sure there are no reinforcements nearby?

~

Dusk seemed in as much a hurry as the army when they made landfall. It quickly doused the evening light while the knights and volunteers assembled in columns along the banks of the seashore.

Ihon was ordered to take a team of three other knights to scout the western end of the fields around the stronghold. He was only glad to do it.

Assembling the team, he urged Seneca forward, the horse's hooves pounding against the hard desert sand.

The scouting party trudged along a rocky trail leading away from the end of the gathering forces. Within a few minutes, they were unable to hear the hundreds of horses neighing and the comotions of troops shouting or bickering.

The desert was a lonely, quiet place.

"I don't believe I would like to live here," one of the three knights spoke up, his raven beard was bespeckled with streaks of gray.

"Too arid, too hot, and too quiet," a younger knight agreed. He was mostly cleanshaven, except for a tuft of brown hair on his chin just below his bottom lip.

Ihon kept his mouth shut, he was too busy using all his supernatural senses to care about where these humans did or did not want to live.

Something echoed on the other side of the rocky hill they were rounding.

Raising his right hand, Ihon motioned for the group to stop. He pointed in the direction of the noise.

A horse snorted — it wasn't one of theirs.

"Should we hide?" The younger knight with the chin tuft questioned, his voice barely above a whisper.

Ihon's nostrils flared, from their odours, he counted five men approaching them. He could also smell hot metal and sweating leather. Did their desert foe wear heavy armour?

"Greetings, friends," the group of five men appeared around the corner. They were dressed in flowing white tunics bearing red crosses across them.

"Templar Knights," the older man with the bespeckled raven beard remarked. "Guardians of the Kingdom of Jerusalem."

"May the Lord our Saviour bless you," one of the Templars smiled, leaning forward in his saddle. "What is your business here?"

Ihon remained stoic. He was remembering a dark memory from the early days of his recruitment the last time he'd been to the Holy Land.

"We've come to capture the city of Acre," the younger knight answered. He was eager to talk with such famed men. He'd likely heard the myths and legends of the Knights Templar who roamed Palestine, protecting pilgrims on their way to Jerusalem. "We're scouting out here to make sure there are no reinforcements for the enemy."

"Ah," one of the Templars nodded. His mouth tightened as he waved a hand over his shoulder. "We caught sight of Saladin's entourage just three miles beyond that mountain to the south."

"Saladin?" Ihon sat up. Feelings of distaste set aside for the moment, he was intrigued. "The Sultan of Egypt and Syria?"

"There very one himself," one of the Templars turned to the leader of the scouts. He raised an eyebrow as he muttered, "You think you could take the man who just captured Jerusalem?"

"By God's Grace," Ihon smirked. "We can do anything. Is that not what it says in the Holy Scriptures?"

The Templars went silent, their looks soured noticeably.

"Will you join us in the coming siege, Sirs?" The young knight was talking again.

"Perhaps," came the response. "We need some food and water, yesternight saw the last of our rations disappear."

"We have more than enough!"

Before Ihon knew what was happening, his entire team had left for the encampment behind them along with the Templar Knights.

"Just as well," he muttered to no one in particular. "I was struggling to keep from lashing out at those Templars." His memory pulled up images of the short time he'd been a member of their ranks.

"They were such a righteous group when first starting out," he spoke to his horse, though he was certain the mount didn't care in the least. "I still wonder to this day who brought in the corruption and greed. Then the satanic rituals that started in a couple branches, that's what forced me out."

He nudged the steed onward down the trail.

"Maybe someday I'll be able to find out the mystery and put them to Justice's sword."

A rock plunged from the edge of a boulder lodged into the side of the mount, clapping against the ground, the echo sounding like two swords clanging together.

Ihon froze.

His dark eyes bounced back and forth along the stony incline's face.

He smelled the human.

Apparently, there was an ambush waiting somewhere above.

18

Hidden eyes boring holes into your back is always the most unsettling of sensations.

Ihon took in the scent of his stalker. Based on the odours, he could tell the human was sweating from possibly a long run.

It was either that or the want-to-be assassin was nervous. Maybe this was his first kill?

The only killing will be of you, Ihon smirked. Though he felt the gaze of the coming attacker, he felt near at ease. Gripping the reins, he waited.

There was the tiniest of scuffles straight above.

"I must give you credit," Ihon muttered loud enough for the ambusher to hear him. "I could barely hear you." Raising his chin, he studied the incline of the boulder.

But before he could lay eyes on the stalker, there was a zip of a whirring noise followed by the smack of a blade into living flesh. Next, a dark shape plummeted behind Ihon and his horse, splattering on the stony path.

Turning Seneca around, Ihon gaped down at the body.

From the height of the fall, it had landed in a twisted, unnatural heap. The limbs were contorted in all the wrong angles and the neck was broken from the way the face was pointing backwards.

A cold finger traced a circle around Ihon's heart.

Those dead eyes stared at him.

"You owe me a thank you, Sir Knight," a familiar voice appraised him.

Ihon looked up to see the blonde knight from the signing tables back in London.

Approaching on a chestnut mare with white spots, the young warrior was carrying a large bow, a satchel of arrows strapped to his back.

"Thank you, young knight," Ihon shrugged. His eyes dropping to the corpse again, he remarked, "The situation was under control."

The blonde man shrugged, pursing his lips. His eyes ran over the body, mouth turning upward.

"You're obviously proud of this," Ihon breathed, eyebrows furrowing.

"Yes," the Englishman broke into a grin. "My first Muslim kill."

"He was a human being like yourself."

"He was about to murder you," the knight raised both eyebrows. "You Scots are all alike, so ungrateful."

"Stupid Englishman, think killing first without asking questions is a good idea," Ihon spat the words. Yes, he was a bit peeved. "For all you know, this assassin could have given us the directions to Saladin's camp. We could have…"

Goose bumps climbed the back of Ihon's neck causing his words to trail off. They turned into tiny prickling needle points tracing his spine and imbedding themselves into his skull.

That scent.

"His Majesty requested every knight to be present at the siege, I came to round you up," the blonde Englishman gave this information as if the insults hadn't even happened. He glared at Ihon, obviously wondering why the older knight was suddenly acting distracted.

Ihon's head swiveled on his neck. He sniffed the air.

The odour was the same.

"What's the matter now?" Growing impatient, the young knight shifted in his saddle.

"Be on your way, I'll follow in a moment," Ihon barely registered his own voice as he waved the warrior away. Nudging Seneca to round the boulder, he sniffed the air again.

Yes, it was the exact same scent. The smell of a Wolf-Born, yet tainted with something that could only be described with one word.

Evil.

"Seneca," Ihon muttered once out of ear shot of the now ranting knight. "I do believe we've discovered our prey. We didn't need the directions from one of his assassins either. Thank God for that discerning scent."

The horse snorted. He obviously wanted nothing to do with this.

Ihon nodded.

Following the incline of the knoll he'd been on, the Wolf-Born Crusader made his way into a ravine about a mile later. Once at the bottom, he brought his mount to a standstill and slipped out of the saddle.

"I'll leave you here, friend," he whispered to the young stallion. "It'll be best I travel on foot anyways. If Elite Rogues can smell just as well as any other Wolf-Born, he'll know you're coming. Of course, he'll most likely smell me coming too. But at least I'll be able to get closer."

With that, he sneaked off into the overhanging shadows.

Thank the Almighty the sun is long since gone down, his mind remarked. Weaving his way under an outcrop of rock, he crouched down and concentrated.

A small growl escaped his lips as his body twisted. Shifting into his Beast form, he nearly slammed his head against the ledge before moving out from under it.

The glow of the moon was in its three-quarters phase, lending light.

Though he had night vision, he was thankful for the extra help.

Ascending the crest of a steppe, Ihon surveyed the land outstretched before him.

Most of it was flat, a few mountainous boulders strewn about—as if some deity had thrown them out like pebbles on a riverbed.

Here and there a small sand devil whirled its way along the desert, thanks to a strong breeze.

Ihon felt the wind rustling his fur, it felt pleasant. But feeling good wasn't on his to-do list at the moment. His dark eyes flashed when they rested on a ring of campfires dotting the desert landscape.

The encampment was near five miles away.

Breaking into a run, Ihon hoped the sound of his padded feet against the rock-drenched sand didn't carry. Tongue curling through his fangs, he charged forward.

"Do you hear that?" A voice rang out in the darkness nearby.

Ihon froze in mid-step. He'd already came within a mile of the camp. Wet nose twitching, he deciphered the distance of the bearer of the voice.

"Sounded like something was hammering those rocks over there," the gruff voice muttered.

Most likely a group of scouts or sentries, Ihon guessed.

They were speaking in Egyptian.

I'm surprised you can understand them, the Wolf-Born thought to himself. But then, your ancestral mother was a princess of Egypt. Perhaps there was something passed down through the genes? He'd have to ask about that once he returned to Sanguiatro.

Lowering himself, he slinked along the edge of another ravine. Following his nose, he located the sentries and crept up behind them.

There were four of them, standing in the ravine, peeking over the edge. Watching the terrain stretching out before them, they shifted on their feet. They were completely oblivious to the monster glaring at them from behind.

"By the gods," the one on the right spoke—he was the same one who spoke first earlier. "You'd think this desert haunted by demons. I cannot wait till our great Sultan sends the outsiders out of Palestine."

"Watch how you speak of our holy leader," the guard next to him spat.

"I meant no disrespect. I simply wish to be home in time for my first child's birth." He leaned up against the ledge.

Ihon was about to take another step toward them when he paused. This last statement made him hesitate. Hand still dangling in the air in mid-stride, he studied the backs of each man.

Maybe he could get past without having to dispatch them.

Backing up, he clenched his fangs together.

"I'm going to check the other side," the soon-to-be father suddenly informed. He turned on his haunches and froze. The whites of his eyes glinted in the moonlight when his gaze fell on the hulking, black-furred demon.

Burning Hades, Ihon's brain swore. He let out a growl, sounding like rumbling thunder.

The other three guards spun on their heels and unsheathed their scimitars.

"By the gods," the fourth was still staring at the Beast. "What is that?"

Ihon could smell the cold sweat now shining across the man's skin. He also caught the scent of a released bladder from the sentry on the left. Baring his fangs, he sent his hackles bristling.

"The Evil One has come in physical form," was the response. "Sound the alar—"

Before the watchman could finish his order, Ihon pushed against his hind legs and leaped. Tackling the guard who'd had the accident with his bodily functions, he smashed him to the ground, closing his giant maw around the bare neck. Clamping down, he gave one quick twist of his head.

The sound of gristle and bone snapping beneath the skin met his large ears.

Flattening those ears, the Wolf-Born turned on the other three.

The first one, the man with the unborn child at home, took off in a desperate run.

Ihon growled again at the remaining two.

They raised their swords.

Brave, the monster thought. But stupid. I'm sorry, men, you were in the wrong place at the wrong time.

"I hope you're ready to meet your Maker," Ihon spoke in his guttural voice.

The shock that registered on the two guard's faces turned their dark skin so pale they could have been ghosts. Their hands trembled as they gripped the hilts of their weapons.

Blood from the first kill drooled down Ihon's chin. He spat it out, snarling. Lifting himself to a standing position, he towered over his opponents. Meeting their gazes, he scowled. Then, in the blink of an eye, he pounced.

Both clawed hands imbedded themselves into both chests of the guards.

Shoving the helpless men to the ground beneath him, Ihon let out a growl as he tore into their chest cavities at the same time. Latching onto their sternums, he leveraged his feet against their abdomens. Raising his head to the sky, he let out a howl as he wrenched the bones out of their sockets.

Warm liquid splattered over his feet.

Ihon dropped his gaze back to the mutilated bodies.

The sounds of boots pounding against the rocks reverberated in his large ears causing them to twitch and turn.

The last sentry was at least a hundred yards away by now.

Not too far, the Beast mused. With a short growl, he took off after his prey.

Gasping for air, the last guard glanced over his shoulder. His heart was racing faster than the beat of a cheetah's chase. The adrenaline pumping through his veins was the only thing keeping his legs working. He could barely breathe as he whimpered.

Saladin's camp was only a few more hundred yards away.

It felt as if it were a million miles away.

The ground started shaking beneath his feet, sending him stumbling.

He was dizzy, head light with so little oxygen on top of the panic that seized him.

The camp was too far.

He'd never make it.

A hideous snarl sent goose bumps up his cold-sweating body.

19

At the sound of that snarl, the guard gasped. So startled, he did not see the loose rock in front of him. The front of his right boot slammed against the rock, sending the rest of his heaving body spiraling face forward against the desert floor.

He sobbed, his hands reaching out. Fingers digging into the sand, he wanted so bad to pull himself up. To make it to the camp, to be free of this nightmare. He longed so much to meet his firstborn child. He wanted badly to live.

The growl overhead froze him. He gagged on the air, his body shivered.

The monster was standing just a foot away from his sprawled form.

Ihon glowered down at his victim. His mind racing, he wondered what to do. His heart beat inside his giant chest, warning him to not step over this invisible line between him and that human being.

But I can't let him return to the camp, his brain argued. He'll give me away before I can get close to Saladin. Then I won't be able to finish my task.

You selfish bastard, his heart snarled. What about him? He misses his family? What about his unborn child? Or his wife? Don't you think they'd miss him? They need him, you unforgiveable, son of a...

Okay, okay, Ihon's mind surrendered. I give in.

Crouching down, the Beast reached out and rested a clawed hand on the calf of the guard's right leg.

The man stiffened but turned his head to look over his shoulder at, what he thought to be, his killer.

"Please," he whimpered. "I have a family." His Egyptian was thick through the snot now pouring down and mixing with his spit.

Ihon nodded his large head, ears flicking forward, no longer in a fighting stance. He motioned for the man to sit up.

Scrambling to his knees, he turned and clasped both hands in a praying position.

"Are you Allah's avenger?" He asked, his eyes pleading. "Will you grant your servant mercy for any wrongs I have done? I ask for mercy and life that I may return to my family."

"I will spare your life," the nightmare rumbled. "As long as you promise not to return to Saladin's camp. I must see you leave for home."

"As you wish, mighty Lord," the man groveled. "I will

never step foot near Saladin again!" With this he jumped to his feet and took off in a run out into the night.

Ihon watched his shape until it disappeared in the shadows of the distant mountains. He then snorted and closed his eyes. Shifting back into human form, he gnashed his teeth as they shrunk into their smaller shapes.

The pungent scent of the Elite Rogue was so much stronger now.

I wonder if he can smell me, Ihon thought. Most likely, he knows I'm here. But why there aren't any scouts, at least, coming out to check, I don't know.

An idea crawled into his mind.

He grimaced. His eyebrows then furrowed, his eyes darting back and forth.

It might work, he mused. Covering myself in their blood might stifle my scent for him. I could probably get a bit closer that way.

Turning back, he strolled over to the torn bodies of the three dead sentries. Dipping his hands in the pools of blood encased in their open chests, he crinkled his nose.

The metallic odour was so strong he could taste it.

Wincing, he dabbed a few streaks on his face then down his arms. Making sure to splatter a bit on his legs and abdomen, he gagged as the warm fumes rose into his nostrils.

"God forgive me," he breathed. Standing up, he slammed his eyes shut. Trying to keep from vomiting, he did an about face and opened his eyes again. Making his way along the ravine, he headed for the encampment.

Most of the warriors had gone to bed for the night, quite a few were tossing and turning inside their tents.

There were a few still awake, sitting around the flickering campfires.

Ihon managed to stay within the shadows of the tents, slipping among them. Once near the center, he caught sight of an extra-colourful pavilion sitting by itself with a ring of smaller fur-skin tents surrounding it.

The light of a fire inside revealed the brawny shadow of a man.

Saladin, Ihon caught the creature's scent over the odour of the smeared blood.

From the shape of the shadows, Saladin was seated at the fire roasting something — it looked like a large animal, maybe a bear or a very large deer.

Creeping up to the pavilion, Ihon was just inches away when he froze.

Saladin's head turned in his direction.

A bead of cold sweat trickled down Ihon's neck.

Standing up, the Sultan trudged over to the flap of the tent that served as its door.

Scurrying off, Ihon dove behind a nearby tent — hoping against hope, he didn't wake the occupant inside. Peeking over the corner, he watched the shape of the Sultan step through and out into the night air.

The blazing fire accentuated his powerful frame, blanketing him in an orange glow.

His shadow dancing against the face of his neighbour's

tent, Saladin stood as still as a statue, the only moving part of his body was his head.

Even from his distance, Ihon could see those ears tensing and the nose flaring. He knew the Elite Rogue was trying to place the familiar smell that was obviously escaping the blood, maybe even locate him. Clenching his teeth, he readied himself, in case he needed to bring on a quick Change.

It seemed like an eternity before Saladin shrugged. Turning to a guard who stood just three yards away, he muttered something.

Ihon's heightened hearing picked up three words from the sentence.

"Make…no…interrupts…" It was obviously a command for no disturbances while he ate his late-night supper.

With that, the Sultan stalked back into the pavilion, his shadow returning to its seat inside. The spit on the fire turned.

Ihon caught a whiff of the roasting meat. Instead of his mouth watering like he expected, he felt a shiver roll across his shoulders as a twinge of bile crept up the back of his throat.

What is it? Ihon raised an eyebrow. He tried not to imagine, disturbed to think the thoughts that were now shooting through his brain might be true.

The minutes ticked by.

Ihon kept his eyes on the figure inside. He watched Saladin hack off a piece of the animal and begin tearing into it with his teeth. Slipping to a near crouch, Ihon moved across the sand back up to the pavilion.

How was he going to get inside and feed the poison? His mind was running a marathon. Thankful he'd kept the tiny vial in a pouch strapped to his arm, he pulled it out. Studying the powder inside, he pursed his lips in deep thought.

"Come on in," Saladin's voice was low. From the sound of it, he was smiling, but it was more the smile an animal gives to warn its foe it has no squabble with biting his head off.

Ihon gritted his teeth. His mind racing, he forced himself to remain calm.

Now's the time for a new plan, he told himself when he reached up and rapped his fingers against the tent wall, letting the pavilion's occupant know where he stood.

There was a brief shuffle then a hand pulled back one of the flaps, revealing Saladin's face inside.

"Hello there," he grinned—looking more like a wolf baring its teeth. "Are you friend or foe?"

"Friend, if you're against the Ancient Creed," Ihon responded, trying his best to keep a friendly mask covering the distaste he felt for this creature.

Slipping inside the tent, the smell of the roasted flesh charged his nostrils just as his eyes took in the sight.

The body tied across the fire spit was not animal—it was human.

Ihon swallowed hard.

His stomach tried to climb up his throat, spilling acid into his mouth.

It was all he could do to keep from vomiting.

Lying on a cushioned cot with dozens of laced satin pillows was a platter holding half an arm, the skin was darkend to a crisp brown while the meat inside was still partially red.

"I like my meat medium rare," Saladin smiled as he took his seat next to the platter, motioning for his guest to sit opposite him on a second couch. "That's what I'm going to call it."

Ihon nodded, trying to keep from blanching at the deplorable sight. He felt a bead of sweat spring on his forehead.

"So," the Sultan spoke through a mouthful of the bite he just took out of the flesh. "What brings you to my tent and why are you covered in blood?"

Keeping as still as possible, trying to force a nonchalant attitude, Ihon responded.

"I heard there was an Elite Rogue in this area," he spun his tale. "I've recently made my parting with the Supreme Council of the Wolf-Borns because I simply don't agree that we should be Law-bound to protect such fickle creatures as these humans. I'd rather eat them then save them."

Saladin's dark eyes twinkled, he picked up a second silver plate and tore off the other arm from the roasted corpse. Handing it to his guest, he smiled.

Ihon raised his right hand — probably a bit too quickly, he thought.

"Thank you," he started. "But, to be honest, I wish my first meal to be killed by myself. Does that make sense?"

The Sultan pursed his lips beneath his thick beard. He then shrugged and nodded.

"As you wish," he set the plate down, leaned back against a stack of pillows, and continued with his meal.

"The blood," Ihon grimaced. "I caught by a couple guards and attacked on instinct. I hope you can forgive."

Saladin broke into a chuckle, waving the hand that wasn't grasping the last bit of meat.

"I can always get more."

"Excellent," Ihon forced a grin. He then leaned forward, eyes landing on a bottle of wine sitting on a small table just a couple feet to his right. "What I would like to do is ask for the honour of pouring us a toast. May I?"

Swallowing the last bite off his plate, the Rogue set the plate down. Bouncing his head up and down, he grinned.

"I love toasts, please do!"

Ihon smiled.

"I do as well, hence why I asked," he responded while reaching out and grabbing the longneck bottle. Setting two golden goblets out on the small table, he poured the drink. Giving a quick flick of his wrist, he grasped the second goblet and stepped over to the Elite, handing it to him.

He has no idea, Ihon mused.

Picking up the goblet he'd poured for himself, he sat back down and raised it in the air.

"To you, to me, and to what could be a new friendship."

"Here here," the Sultan raised the cup. His gaze honed in on Ihon's eyes.

There was something there.

Ihon caught himself before narrowing his eyes, trying to figure out what that look was revealing. Did the Rogue suddenly become aware of the trick?

Surely he couldn't smell the Hemlace juice? Ihon's mind began to race. What if becoming Rogue empowered your already inhuman senses? What if this was about to break out into a bloodbath that Ihon would most likely lose — seeing as he did not have as much experience as this five-hundred-year-old Elite Rogue carried.

Noran had informed Ihon of this right before he'd left, warning him of the cunning this monster held.

But then, Saladin gulped the drink down.

Raising his eyebrows, Ihon rolled his shoulders.

"What?" Saladin caught the movement, bringing the cup down away from his face. His eyes flashed.

"I was just surprised," Ihon stated. "You are more trusting than I expected."

Saladin opened his mouth, revealing fangs. His body was beginning to change into Beast form. Shoulders pulled back, neck forward, he stood to his feet.

"You think you could poison me?" The Elite Rogue growled. "I didn't become Elite for no reason."

"So," Ihon jumped up, facing off with the shifting monster. "Hemlace juice no longer affects us once we've gone Rogue?"

The Sultan's eyes bulged.

At first, Ihon thought it was an effect of the Change.

Then it dawned on him, there was real fear in those wide eyes.

"Hemlace juice?" Saladin bellowed. "How did you know about—"

His throat constricted, gagging him here.

"How did I know about Hemlace juice?" Ihon grinned. "I'm an officer of the Creed—all officers know about that weakness. Saladin, you have been weighed in Justice's balances and been found lacking. You have broken the laws of the Ancient Creed, defied God Almighty and the Supreme Council of the Wolf-Born Race. The Supreme Council has found you guilty and condemned you to death. I am your executioner."

"How dare you," Saladin managed to rasp out, collapsing to his knees. The Change had stopped at this point, leaving him halfway between human and Beast forms—he looked like a demon from Hell itself.

Jaws misaligned, fangs protruded at different angles, spit and blood drizzling down his lips, the creature choked. He rocked back on his haunches once then leaned forward, face to the ground.

"You…die…" his voice was a mangled mess of slobbering. "For this."

Ihon stared, the scene was too gripping to look away. Icy tendrils crawled up his arms, turning into tiny needles prickling the back of his neck.

A growl escaped the creature's gaping mouth, turning into a hiss as he toppled over onto his side. His neck unclenching, Saladin shook for about five seconds before going still. Head lolling to the side, his eyes froze open.

Ihon was almost certain he could hear the spirit screaming as it was dragged from the corpse down to the pits of torment in the next world after this.

"Your Highness," a voice clammered outside the front tent flap. There was a rustle and the guard who'd been standing outside, rushed in. "I heard something, are you all right?"

Ihon glared at the human.

The guard came to an abrupt halt, his hands gripping the spear he was holding. Gaze dropping to the lifeless creature on the ground then lifting to the stranger standing over it, he opened his mouth to say something.

20

The look on the guard's face showed he had no idea what to say. It was as if he'd stumbled in on his own nightmare. Next thing he knew, the stranger was overpowering him.

Ihon tore the spear out of the guard's hands, tossing it away. He then clutched the man by the neck of his frock and leaned in.

"You will not breathe a word," the Crusader snarled, eyes only inches away from the guard's ashen face. "You see the monster your Sultan was? I can turn into something far more hideous—if you speak of this to anyone else. Do I make myself clear?"

The sentry sniveled. His eyes were glued to the hideous corpse.

It was then that it started to dissipate into a pile of ash.

Ihon shook him, turning his attention to him.

"You do! I won't," the guard sobbed. He shut his eyes— mind most likely imagining so many variations of a horrendous death.

"Good job," Ihon let go his grasp. "Now," he brushed the wrinkles out of the tunic. "You will obey whatever I command you."

The guard nodded.

"What's your name?"

"Muha-tin," the man, trembling all over, knelt down in front of the stranger.

"Well," Ihon sneered down. "Muha-tin, you're going to be Saladin."

"What?" The prisoner raised his head, eyes wider than it could be thought possible.

"You're going to masquerade as your former Sultan and help me bring an end to this war. King Richard of the Holy Crusade is capturing your stronghold at Acre. I want, after the siege, for you to send word to him that you wish to parlay and discuss a treaty."

Muha-tin stared at him, this news was obviously overwhelming and his brain was working in overdrive to comprehend it.

"Do you think you could pull it off?" Ihon leaned down, making eye contact again. "Or should I find someone else?"

"No, Master," Muha-tin shook his head so violently, Ihon was certain it might twist off. "But there are several among the ranks that would recognise me."

"That's easy," Ihon waved a hand as he approached the tent door. "No one will be allowed to come in here, except for the foreigners when I summon them to discuss the treaty."

Muha-tin nodded. He suddenly felt like his entire frame had taken on a thousand pounds. Eyes falling to the couch, he struggled to keep from crumpling to the floor.

Ihon noticed this and motioned for the man to sit down. No reason to have a passed out fake-Saladin on his hands in case more guards showed for check up.

Muha-tin dropped onto the couch like a sack of potatoes, his arms stretched out. He was shocked at how taxing the terror of just a few minutes could take on his body. As soon as this ordeal was over, if he lived through it, he really needed to find a better exercise routine.

After morning's light stretched across the sky and Ihon had sneaked out of the camp, passing word to King Richard, informing him of the Saladin's wish for a treaty of peace — the arrangements were made.

Returning to the pavilion, Ihon was cautious, every one of his supernatural senses attuned to any form of disturbance within the campsite. Slipping inside, he laid eyes on the slumbering form of Muha-tin.

The guard had changed into one of the former Sultan's robes and wrapped a turban around his head. He now lay sprawled out on the couch where Saladin had been eating supper.

The roasted corpse was still hanging above the fire.

Grimacing, Ihon growled. He could not understand how anyone could sleep with such a hideous sight just a yard away from them.

The metal clashed against the ring of stones surrounding the dying fire as Ihon picked up the spit with the corpse.

"I am awake," Muha-tin snapped to an upright posture. His glazed eyes widened at the sight of the assassin back in the tent.

Ihon gave another growl—even in human form, it seemed natural. He tossed the cadaver through the back flap of the tent. Turning around, his dark eyes rested on the new Sultan.

"King Richard will be here with in the hour, are you ready?"

"I am, Master," the guard was eager to please. "What shall I say?"

"Not much," Ihon took a few steps toward his prisoner. "The Englishman doesn't speak Egyptian or Arabic so I will pretend to interpret for you. You just pretend to be discussing the details of the treaty."

"Master," the guard dropped his eyes to the ground. "My people cannot suffer. Please don't make us."

"Don't worry," Ihon felt the twitch of a smirk at the edges of his mouth. "I'll make it as fair as possible. Your people have already done quite a bit of damage. Of course, so have the ones who call themselves Christians—though, many of their actions are not very Christ-like. But, all I wish for is peace."

Muha-tin bobbed his head.

The hour passed and Richard arrived.

No one except for the King and one of his servants was allowed inside the pavilion. Everyone else remained outside, glaring at each other.

With Ihon leading the discussion, King Richard surprised by the unexpected open-mindedness of his foe, and the fake-Sultan's ramblings just to appear as if he were making the discussions, the signing of the treaty went quite well.

The entire time though, Ihon's mind was already turning back to Scotland and the Capitol of his People there. How he could not wait to return.

He was thankful, Richard did not recognise him. This would make sense, with how many men the King met in a single day alone.

Once the treaty was written and signed, both parties separating on a friendlier term, Ihon watched as the English King departed for his own camp. He smiled through the open flap of the pavilion. Then, turning back around to face Muha-tin, he nodded.

"You did well," he admitted, picking up a satchel. He strung the small bag over his shoulder and headed for the door.

"Where are you going?" The fake-Saladin called after him.

"My job here is done," the assassin replied. "But, if you do decide to go back on the treaty you just signed, remember, it may have been ink you put down, but it was with your life's blood." He gave a stern stare then vanished out the door.

Muha-tin swallowed the acid that jumped into the back of his throat. He then shut his eyes and shivered.

～

Deciding not to wait for the Crusading forces' departure, Ihon grabbed his horse from the camp during the first night back in the friendly camp. He slipped off and reached the northernmost tip of the Kingdom of Jerusalem by sunrise.

The weeks passed as the rider and his stallion traveled up across Turkey, seeing the site where the very first Sanguiatro was built, then passing into the European continent on their way to the English Channel.

Anxious to get back, Ihon decided to save the visit to the second site of the Capitol near Rome for a later date.

At Seneca's pace, they arrived at the Channel on the third day of the fourth month since leaving the Holy Land. It took three days to get across by ship, then less than a week to finally enter the Highlands of Scotland.

"We're almost there, boy," Ihon grinned down at his mount, his right hand patting the strong neck of the battle steed. "After this, perhaps it would be best I travel to distant lands on my own, don't want to age you too fast."

Seneca snorted.

As the familiar mountain came into view, Ihon smiled. It was strange when that sentimental emotion overpowered you, making you feel as if certain memories had taken place simultaneously in yesterday and a hundred years ago.

A hundred years ago, Ihon thought. I'm not that quite old yet. Can't believe I've got less than twenty years to go—and I still feel like I'm in my prime!

The sun trudged down the sky, the moon on his tail.

Like two lovers, always chasing each other. Some evenings or mornings they came so close, yet still so far.

Could I ever find love again? Ihon wondered. He felt a pang of guilt at the thought, his mind trailing back to Joanna. He hadn't returned to their old stone house since leaving it over thirty years ago.

It was strange how it felt so much like a totally different life back then.

Come to think of it, it kind of was a different life. Back then, he still thought he was human. He had a human wife—a human life.

I wonder if there is a woman of the Wolf-Borns who could measure up to you, my love. Ihon's mind was so busy reminiscing and pondering such questions, he barely noticed when Seneca pranced into town down the main street.

"Sir Ihon," a voice cut into his thoughts.

His head whirling to the right, he rested his eyes on the familiar face of Bhaltair. It felt like years since he'd last seen that face.

"Great days of old," Ihon jumped from his horse and opened his arms wide as the white-bearded man charged up to him.

They clapped each other on the back as they laughed.

"Good to see you, old man," Ihon grinned.

"Whose old? I still feel spry and young like you, boy," Bhaltair winked—his eyes said otherwise, the obvious sign of exhaustion etched in around them.

"What have you been conniving since I left?"

"Seeing the world, seeing the world," the Supreme Councilman ran his right hand through his long white hair.

Clasping his horse's reins, Ihon started up the road to the Keep, his friend at his side.

"I wanted to see the place where the Father of our Race gave the gift to our Mother. Down there in Egypt, you know?"

"Aye," Ihon nodded. "Did you find it?"

"Aye, that I did," the elder grinned, eyes growing distant. "The feeling was not what I expected."

"What was it like?" Ihon stared up the road.

"Dark," the Councilman grimaced. "Evil. Like Satan himself had made it his abode. I guess the story is true about it also being the birth place of the Spawn."

"Intriguing," the younger Wolf-Born tilted his head.

Finally reaching the gates of the Keep, they were let in by the guards and Ihon took his horse to the stable in the back of the courtyard. Before he returned to his home in the city, he needed to inform the rest of the Council of his successful mission.

The two were greeted by Merryn who wore a brilliant smile.

"Welcome back, both of you."

Ihon glanced at Bhaltair.

"Aye," the elder smiled. "I just got back last night but have been stalling coming up here. Guess I was just enjoying the socialising with the folks, I hadn't gotten around to it."

"Well," Ihon winked. "You are the eldest Councilman, I would think you could take your time if you wanted to."

"And he did," Merryn gave an annoyed glance in jest. She then winked at Ihon while petting Bhaltair on the arm. She then cleared her throat as another member joined the group.

It was Noran.

"Ihon, you've returned," the Chief greeted the officer.

"Mission was a success," Ihon nodded. "Saladin's ashes are soaring invisibly on the desert wind. I put an imposter in his place, he and King Richard of England, in fact, signed a treaty of peace before I left."

"Sounds like good news," Noran pursed his lips. "I wonder how long that'll last before the world is plunged into yet another of those pointless Crusades."

"Pointless?" Bhaltair cocked an eyebrow.

"This was the third in not even two centuries. Squabbles over a piece of land, slaughtering thousands, it just seems pointless to me."

"It didn't seem pointless to those who gave their lives," Ihon spoke up. He cleared his throat before finishing, "Sir."

Bhaltair smirked at him. Then with a deep breath, he muttered.

"Well, I'm famished from my trip, there's going to be a feast tonight at my neighbours. You are all invited of course."

"I'm exhausted," Ihon raised both eyebrows. "Thank you for the offer, but I would prefer a long rest."

Noran nodded, "Has anyone told you of the Haven?"

"Haven?" Ihon questioned.

"Aye," Merryn grinned. Her eyes grew distant.

"Yes," Noran answered. "It's a place actually built for Wolf-Borns if they wish to take a vacation from this life. The time passes differently there, you can spend a day and return to find a century has passed, giving you the equal amount of rest. You return completely revived."

"Not to mention the Haven is like a piece of Paradise itself," Merryn remarked.

"Where is it?" Ihon lifted an eyebrow.

The two escorted him back to the front door of the Keep and outside. They slipped around the round black-brick structure. Upon reaching a corner where the wall met the rock face of the mountain, they pointed to a small door and informed him.

"If you take the path beyond that door, it will lead you down the other side of our mountain, across a small valley with one of the brooks that feed our lake," Noran began.

Merryn continued for him. "Beyond that, there is a second mountain, about two thirds of the way up a very clear path, you'll find an old tree growing out of the rock itself. Beneath its roots, you'll see the mouth of a cave. The Haven is in there."

Ihon stared at them for a moment.

"I can just go there now? I don't need to pack anything?"

"No," Merryn smiled. "Like we said, the time passes differently. The food there is delicious too, the hostess usually provides it at a large table—though most never even lay eyes on her during their stays. Those who have seen her—always only from a great distance—are blessed beyond compare."

"Sounds like a goddess," Ihon mused.

"Not exactly," Merryn giggled. "But then again, somewhat."

"What do you mean?"

"She's an Immortal."

"What's an Immortal?"

Merryn's eyes twinkled. She glanced at Noran.

"It's a long story," he remarked. "And the sun is sinking low. You should head there now. We'll see you in a century or two." He chuckled, waved goodbye, and headed back to the Keep.

"Enjoy your time," Merryn waved goodbye.

Ihon watched them go.

Well, that was thoughtful of them, he shook his head. Glancing at the door in the wall, he narrowed his eyes and bit his bottom lip.

They just showed him a mystery, everything in his gut wanted to unravel it.

Stepping through the door, he studied the grassy path before him.

"Down the mountain, across the stream, and up another mountain to an old tree growing out of stone," he repeated to himself. Following the trail until he came around the corner of the mountain, he came to a halt.

The view was incredible.

He could see for miles, the mountains of Scotland greeting him like friendly giants from ancient yore.

There were forests on both sides, but the path cut through a meadow that ran down the incline to a gurgling stream which was only about five feet across. The meadow then climbed up to the halfway zone of the second mountain before it turned into a gray cliff. But even from this distance, Ihon could make out the thin line of the trail zigzagging up the bluff.

And there was the tree.

"Might as well," Ihon shrugged. He found himself trotting down the path and in minutes, he was at the tree gaping at the hulking roots that spread out like tentacles before diving into the rock.

Formed by, what appeared to be, the natural growth of the roots, a cave mouth yawned.

Ihon stepped into the shadows — the sun had just dipped its bottom to the horizon outside, so the darkness was already climbing the peak. But, with his night vision, the Wolf-Born made his way down the tunnel.

An evening breeze managed to seep through the overhanging roots and whistle in between a couple stalagmites a few feet away.

His moccasins crunched against the pebble-strewn floor while he meandered through the darkness.

The hair on the back of his neck stood up.

For one brief moment, it sounded as if the wind snapped its fingers.

Then Ihon was standing in the middle of a garden. He froze.

"What under the sun," he mumbled. Spinning on his heels, he saw only the wide trunk of a hollowed tree where he was certain a cave should be. His mouth dropped open, eyes widening.

The colours came from every hue of the rainbow and in between — quite possibly, even more.

Pink cherry trees welcomed him like familial guardians. Shrubs and bushes with every species of roses, peonies, and various flowers he could not recognise, dotted the ground.

The grass was everywhere, greener than any Scottish meadow he'd ever laid eyes on. The blues and purples of heather blanketed the edges of the trail where he stood — it was made of smooth-faced stones coloured several different shades of red.

Ihon felt his arms tingle, sending a shiver all the way down to his wrists. He started to gasp for air, his heart was beating faster than a wild cat could run.

So much light!

So many colours!

This was so unearthly, for a creature of supernatural heritage. For a being who preferred the night, the glimmering rays of sunshine streaming down through the branches above were almost too much.

Yes, it was all extravagant — such beauty would send anyone madly into love with the place.

No wonder Merryn had called it Paradise.

Ihon broke into a run. He could feel the change coming on. Feeling as if he needed to find shelter — or at least a shady spot—he stalked through the colourful underbrush. His heart pounding, he tore into an orchard.

The grass around the twenty or so fruit trees was already sprinkled with petals from the blossoms drenching the branches.

He smelled water.

Nostrils flaring, he charged out of the orchard and over a steep hill. As soon as he made the crest, his feet froze, nearly throwing himself headlong into the clear lazy water of a small lake. Dark eyes growing so wide the moon would be jealous, he gaped.

A voluptuous figure rose out of the waters. While the water cascading down her body, she reached for a flowing laced robe and donned it.

Every single cell in Ihon's body felt as if it were on fire, he could feel his bones beginning to contort in preparation for the Change.

A growl rumbled from the back of his throat, reverberating across his tongue and out between his teeth.

The woman lifted her head from tying the robe at her waist. Her eyes landed on him and she went as still as a statue.

Ihon could not tear his gaze away from hers.

Those eyes, they would melt the heart of the coldest miser. Honey brown with sparks of emerald, they cut right into your very soul—making you want to bare your self to this being as if that would give you the answer to the universe.

Ihon's breath was stolen.

His legs lost their strength and he went down on his knees.

This was too much for him — this place, this goddess.

His eyes to the ground, he felt the rumble in his chest again.

Shoulders rolling, his bones started to realign.

A hand touched his right shoulder and rested there.

His glance, grasping for something to hold onto, found those heavenly eyes and clung to their soft warmth as if for dear life.

Her face, the colour of baked cream, was only inches away.

"It's all right," her voice filled his ears, sending prickling tickles down the sides of his neck. "Just breathe."

Ihon inhaled, realising he hadn't done that in quite a moment. Exhaling then inhaling again, he was certain the calming affect was emanating from the touch of her soft hand on his shoulder.

In less than a minute, his body returned to human form.

Ihon found himself smiling, still dazed by her beauty.

The locks of her hair waved down to her upper thighs, their colour reminded Ihon of smoldering embers.

"Are you the Immortal I was told about?"

She smiled.

Ihon caught his breath again. He'd never seen such a wide smile, revealing perfect, white teeth, stirring a new thrill in his bones.

"What's your name?" He found himself asking, voice barely above a whisper.

Eyes twinkling, she stood upright, taking her hand off his shoulder. She glanced around as if expecting someone to be eavesdropping.

Ihon waited, never taking his eyes off of her for even a split second.

She turned back to him and dazzled him again with that smile before finally answering.

"I'm Zandra."

COMING IN JANUARY 2020:

LONGEVITY: INDEPENDENCE

BY JOHN IRVIN

JOHN IRVIN

If you enjoyed this book please go to its link on Amazon and write a review. You can also find more of John Irvin's works at his Amazon Author Page at amazon.com/author/irvinnovelist76

John Irvin lives in Florida. He graduated college with a Bachelor of Arts degree in Humanities in 2013. John took up writing during his high school days, writing several short science-fiction and fantasy books. He enjoys reading all genres and studying nature or history in his spare time. Besides being a full-time speculative fiction novelist, as he likes to call himself, John also offers his services as a free-lance writer.

If you would like to contact him:

john@johnirvinauthor.com

Website: johnirvinauthor.com

www.ingramcontent.com/pod-product-compliance
Lightning Source LLC
Chambersburg PA
CBHW021157110726
47900CB00002B/622